AN ARTIST

of

DARING CREATIVITY

Micheline Bousquet

An Analytical Biography

NORMAN BEAUPRÉ

An Artist of Daring Creativity
Copyright ©2022 by Norman Beaupré

ISBN: 978-1-951901-64-6   [Paperback Edition]
      978-1-951901-65-3   [eBook Edition]

For Monique and Mia----ne l'oubliez jamais/never forget her

Chapter ONE :

A SERENDIPITOUS MEETING OF MINDS
AND HEARTS

I FIRST MET Micheline Bousquet through an affiliation with her mother. I had advertised in the local papers a Winter Term offering, January 1985, sponsored by the University of New England in Biddeford, Maine, a course entitled "Impressionism and French Artists." It was a course   designed to travel to France and study in three weeks time selected artists such as Renoir, Monet and Pissarro. I had already created and offered a full semester course on French Impressionism after having travelled to Paris several times and gathered information on the subject. Having visited museums such as the Jeu de Paume and later the revamped Gare d'Orsay known as the Musée d'Orsay, I had developed a working knowledge of the Impressionist movement in art. Although my academic skills were honed in the realm of French literature having received a doctorate in this field of study, I had developed a keen interest as well as an insightful awareness of French Impressionism, enough to dare explore the challenges of a full course offering. My Humanities department allowed such academic adventures especially when it came to Winter Terms. Winter Terms were consecrated to a single course especially a course outside the regular offerings, and one that involved travel in order to stimulate students in exploring other cultures, artistic values and historical features. Such a course was one that was offered by Professor Jacques Downs whose specialty was history. He offered a course in Mexico. Others such as a biol-

1

ogy teacher offered a course in Belize while another offered one in Alaska. I thought I would challenge students to participate in my course offering while stimulating them with the chance to travel to France. Besides, I truly wanted to return to France myself.

Unfortunately, I only had three students who signed up for my course. I was about to cancel it when the idea came to me to open it up to people in the local communities who wished to travel to France and learn more about French Impressionists. One morning, I received a call from a lady who introduced herself as Madame Bousquet. She wanted to inform me about her daughter, Micheline, who was living in southern France and was an artist herself. She had read in my advertisement that I would be going to Renoir's home in Cagnes-sur-Mer now a museum. I told her that I most probably would take advantage of the occasion to get together with her daughter once there. I wanted indeed to meet her daughter since it would offer me some insights into Provence and share that with my students. I got the detailed information about Micheline Bousquet from the mother while she was going to inform her daughter of my arrival in Nice. I thanked her and proceeded to try and recruit other participants in my course. I got one other person, a senior woman who had wanted to experience what I was offering but had not had the chance to do so. She jumped at the occasion since it meant going with a small group. With her inclusion, I was able to offer my course since the number had jumped to four which meant that I was able to meet the basic requirement of numbers of adherents to a Winter Term offering. The lady's name was Mrs. Bourque. She told me that her middle name was Églantine, a name for a particular rose.

I received a large card with a watercolor design dated January 2, 1985 from Micheline Bousquet telling me, "As things go here, I'm a bit late in responding to your note of last Oct.25th...I would be very pleased to meet with your group and yourself soon upon your arrival & would hope your itinerary is flexible enough so that we can arrange this. I'm gathering for you at present detailed information on your specific questions & will provide you with this list as soon as possible or on your arrival." She gave me her phone number and told me to call her when I got to Nice. I found her to be very cordial and cooperative.

Having succeeded in the official implementation of my Winter Term course, I was prepared to follow my syllabus and start the course in Paris with a visit to the Musée d'Orsay. Once established in our hotel, the five of us directed ourselves to the Rue de Lille having taken the Metro, Solferino. The students as well as Mrs. Bourque were tired and sleepy, but I told them that they would rest up that night and there was no time to waste sleeping. "Stay alert and awake," I told them, "and enjoy your first experience among the giants of art especially the Impressionists." Rest and sleep would come that night as no one wanted to step out. They all followed me and my advice as well as the cogent information I had prepared for them. We studied such works as Monet's "Les Coquelicots d'Argenteuil", Pissarro's "La pastorella," and Berthe Morisot's "Le berceau." I made sure to look at one of Renoir's paintings, "Jeunes filles au piano"and I insisted that they recognize the brightness and clarity of light in the painting. Monet's painting displayed an embankment of tall grasses and red poppies with a small boy following most probably his mother who carries a parasol. It's truly a plein air painting. The Pissarro painting has a young girl sitting on the banks of some outdoor setting. She wears a common blue apron over her peasant dress and is holding a long stick in her left hand. She appears to be in a daydream. A true pastoral scene. As for the cradle painting of Berthe Morisot, it's a delightful scene of a quiet moment when a mother watches over her young child sleeping under a lace veil in its cradle. There is an aura of peace and tranquility there. Renoir's painting shows two young girls, one sitting at a piano with long radiant and lush blond hair while the other girl with darker hair is looking over the music sheet. I told the students to bear in mind the luminosity and gay atmosphere for which Renoir is noted. They all seemed impressed by what they saw and I was so glad we were at this particular museum. The renovated train station caught everyone's eye since we all thought it was a delight as well as an architectural wonder. We were told that thousands upon thousands visited the museum each year. Even today, it's one of the most visited art museums in the world. We stayed three days in Paris and then took the train to Nice. Mrs. Bourque blended in very well with the students and was enjoying herself. I was pleased and looked forward to going down south and eventually meet Micheline Bousquet whose mother had kept insisting I spend some time with her.

We took the train around noon and arrived in Nice refreshed and eager to settle into our rooms at the hotel. Once we got settled in some students wanted to stroll along the beach. I let them get some fresh air and some exercise for their weary legs. I wasn't able to reach Micheline at the number that was given to me since I then realized that she must be at work in Monaco at the Oceanographic Museum affiliated with the well-known ocean explorer and scientist Jacques-Yves Cousteau where she worked as an interpreter. Micheline's mother had told me about her daughter's job. I called Micheline later and I was able to make a rendez-vous with her at our hotel. I found her very nice and accommodating. I planned to have a rosée wine and cake for her reception with our group the following evening. That evening, I let the students relax and explore the surroundings while I did some further investigation of possible side trips while we were there. I knew I wanted to bring the group to Cagnes-sur-mer to visit Renoir's house. I would do that the following morning right after breakfast.

We got up early the following day and boarded a bus to go to Renoir's house. We got there and everything was very quiet if not deserted. To my great disappointment the house was closed to visitors. They were doing some repairs and I had chosen a date and a time that were not fortunate for my plans. We walked around the property but there wasn't much to see. There was no indication when Renoir's house would reopen. We returned to our hotel. Some students took a nap while others went

4

shopping. Mrs. Bourque went strolling on the beach. I talked to the one in charge of the dining facility about our small reception for Micheline and he told me that all would be ready on time that evening. I would remind the group before dinnertime about our encounter with the artist and that I expected everyone to be there. Not everyone had dinner at the hotel that night. Some had found their own delightful place for pizza and other food that they preferred. I wanted to give them as much freedom as possible to choose whenever and whatever except that they had to be at the reception of Micheline Bousquet.

Micheline arrived on time and displayed a sense of charm and warmth that I found alluring. She talked about her skills as an artist and her art work. She remained with me after the students left. We chatted about Maine and other topics that came up. She was glad to meet someone from "home" she said and she shared her experiences of moving to France in 1980 where she was convinced that her success as an artist would materialize. She had chosen France because French was her maternal language and the south of France since it would be warmer than the northern part as well as the cold New England weather in the winter months that she had known.

We finished the course in France and flew back to the States in the dead of winter. It was cold and blustery, the usual weather in New England in wintertime. The semester ended in May and following graduation most students went home for the summer months. Mrs. Bourque got in touch with me telling me that she had truly enjoyed the course and the travel to France. She especially enjoyed meeting Micheline, she said. She really liked her skills as an artist and the way she explained her work specifically in watercolor. The students did not talk too much about their experience in France but they had enjoyed the art works they had seen. In the meantime, I received a letter from Micheline telling me that she had truly enjoyed our conversation at the restaurant in Nice and that she invited me to go and see her if I ever went back to southern France. I wrote back telling her that I sincerely wanted to return to France and to her place in Saint-

Jean-Cap-Ferrat and have friendly conversations with her if I ever had the opportunity to do so. Saint-Jean-Cap-Ferrat was a small commune in Southeastern France. It was located on a peninsula in the heart of the French Riviera between Nice and Monaco. Somehow, Micheline and her two daughters had landed there after they left the States. I felt that I had made a friend. Art was a true venue for me, an opening of the mind and heart. Being creative was a true path in life for me and I believed that it was the same for Micheline the artist. We had connected. We were on the path of sharing our feelings and thoughts on how creativity enriched one's life. She told me that many people had told her earnestly that she should get a real job in order to earn a living. She had very few resources especially in funds. I suspected that she was poor, not indigent, but poor although she was very resourceful and tried sincerely to find means of earning enough to support her two children and her art work. Special paper, watercolors and brushes cost a lot. Somehow she managed. She never begged me for money. She drove an old volkswagen and got around the village where she lived without asking for help. She was determined to survive on her own. Eventually, she left her job at the Oceanographic Museum and devoted most of her efforts to her watercolors. She did not have to pay for school for her two girls since everything was paid for by the government. Many things were part of the benefits afforded by a society-friendly government. She had free living quarters given to her by two sisters who took a liking to her and her two girls. Micheline ran errands and did many favors for them. Although the two girls did not speak French at first, they were quick to learn the native language once they were immersed in the French culture. They had to learn in order to live there effectively and without too many problems. They did it fast enough given the fact of cultural immersion. They remained bilingual for quite a while. Today they only speak French. These girls always felt that they had been abandoned by their father whom they called "l'Américain." Micheline never talked about him but I understood that he was quite the odd fellow who never quite connected with Micheline and the two girls. There seemed to be a cold and distant relationship between them. Later on, I found out that he had visited them only once in France after he had gotten remarried to someone Micheline did not know. He had only given meager child support but no alimony so that Micheline had to struggle all of her life after the divorce. She got rid of her married name for her benefit and that of her children, she told me. Besides, she wanted her French name if she was going to live in France.

As the months flew by, I kept receiving news about Micheline and her efforts to survive in France. Nevertheless, she was Francophone and could speak French fluently although she had to learn many new twists of the language especially some vocabulary and the many expressions and idioms she did not know. She used to tell me that the French people thought she was "la petite cousine canadienne" due to her accent. I told her once that she was not Canadian and she should tell people so. She was an American Francophone whose maternal language was French. The French people could not understand that there were some Americans like myself and Micheline who could speak French fluently. It was, after all, our maternal language. Quite often when I returned to France, I was told that they knew I was not Parisian on account of my accent, but was I Swiss, Belgian, certainly not Québécois since I did not reveal that accent in my speech, they said. "Non, je suis Américain" I used to tell them. They could not believe that an American could speak French fluently. They had that stereotype in mind, an American who only knew one language, English, and oftentimes murdered the French language whenever they tried to speak French. The é, accent aigu, became "ay" and the u became "ou." Micheline eventually mastered the language of her ancestors and was able to communicate very well, as well as any native French woman.

With time Micheline and I forge ahead with our relationship as friends and creators of art and language. We even considered a summer seminar while she lived in Varengeville-sur-mer in Normandy. This seminar would involve comparing Micheline's creative effort in art while I would deal with my writing and publishing as a creative effort to express art in words. We would try to show how to live art as an expression of the soul in gestation trying to find the right way to explain our "raison d'être" as artists and our determination to impart it on others who seek their own reason for being. It never materialized.

When I was in Nice and Micheline had moved from her little apartment that was owned by the two sisters and was staying with her friends, Ben and Janine, a couple who worked with her in Monaco, I took advantage of the situation and asked Micheline if I could interview her on tape. She consented and I still have that tape recording. Incidentally. Micheline had had some misunderstanding with one of the two sisters, if not an altercation of some sort, and one of them had hit Micheline on the chest which led to their separation. Micheline was hurt by this and tried to brush off the entire incident without bad thoughts and feelings of vengeance. Micheline, as far as I could see, was a peace-loving and non-violent type of a person. She would never feel seriously offended nor would she seek retaliation for any offenses that most people would find resentful. She always tried to mitigate any dire situation that came her way. She would try to talk her way out of a disturbing situation rather that fight it out. As she once told me, she was a rebel at heart but not a fistfight fighter. I was always impressed by her manner of handling any situation be it one that showed temerity of soul or one that invited rancor and revenge. It seemed to me that she turned most of her feelings and maligned sense of being who she was in the expression of her art. Art for her was a challenge and a venue for creative efforts that stimulated her desire to impart her sense of well-being with self and others. Art for her transformed any misunderstanding or rift that came her way and made them the challenge that stimulated her creative energies. The only challenge that she could not meet nor fully understand was the fact that her art did not sell. She tried ever so hard in so many directions and the whole question of marketing and publicizing her work fell through for her. That she never understood. She could not fathom the reasons behind her failure to attract buyers.

She told me once that she would be willing to hand over most of her profits to a good marketing agent that could effectively publicize and sell her paintings. She never found one.

However that's only part of Micheline's life as an artist. I want to go deeper inside her heart and soul, the creative artist that she was as well as the woman and mother that she revealed by her actions and thoughts. She certainly was a woman of ideals and dreams. Nevertheless, she was a true realist and objective individual while remaining a person of genuine feelings. She accepted certain rules in life but also rejected others that hindered her sense of integrity and willful enthusiasm. She did not like people who lived by strict moral standards and who imposed them on other people without bearing in mind that people are different and wish to remain loyal to their own standards of life. She found religions often too strict and coercive, too daunting and at times offensive. She did not like to live in a mold only to be cast aside by those who molded and disfigured the person that was. She would rather leave everyone to their own standards and not force anyone to maintain rigidity and coercive factors. She would never deprive any person of choices. Choices were made to bolster and define one and not remove the person from a sense of freedom and choice. Micheline strongly believed in the right to explore the many choices that one had as a human being. All she really cared for in raising her two girls was that they would become women of integrity and self-sufficiency. Most of all, she wanted them to be happy in life and self-fulfilled in their quest for being creative and successful in whatever endeavor they chose as a profession or job. She was not a domineering mother nor was she a domineering friend. She allowed me to be who I truly was and truly felt. I could easily and comfortably confide in her any thoughts or desires that filled my heart and my mind and I would do so willingly and freely without any remorse. To me that was the acid test of being a true friend. Compatibility and compassion were the two words that I would use to describe any good relationship in any given friendship. Micheline offered me both with fierté and understanding. That is the reason why I considered her my best friend.

I understood her and she understood me. Well, the time has come for me to put together all of my notes, emails and letters dealing with Micheline the artist and reveal to the reader what made her the artist she truly was.

Chapter TWO:

FORMATION OF THE ARTIST

MY FIRST INTERVIEW with Micheline occurred on December 11, 1986 at the end of my first sabbatical in Paris. The rent on my studio apartment on rue Chevreuse expired at the end of November and my sabbatical ended the last week of December. I was due to re-turn to the University and pick up my teaching assignment for the Spring semester in January. I took the opportunity to go and visit Micheline in St-Jean-Cap-Ferrat for two weeks before going home. However, she was now living temporarily with two friends, husband and wife, who lived in a two-bedroom apartment in Nice. When I arrived in Nice by train(I had to take a later train than that which I had told Micheline I would take due to changes of scheduling) I had no one to meet me at the gare. I waited and waited until I realized it was getting late, and so I took a taxi to go to Micheline's residence telling myself I would meet her there somehow. I got out of the cab, paid the taxi driver took my luggage and knocked on the door of the address that Micheline had given me. No response. Everything was quiet and somewhat deserted. I was terribly surprised. I waited on the small porch for about an hour. It was cold. After all, it was December. I did not know what to do. I crouched on the floor of the small porch tell-ing myself I would sleep there until I could reach my friend early in the morning. It was around one o'clock in the early hours of the morning. Then to my surprise a young man came to see me and offered me a room in one of the rental apartments that he cared for telling me that Madame Bousquet was no longer inhabiting the residence of the ladies who owned it. Where was she, I asked. He did not know. He was very kind to make that offer. The room had not been rented and so he took the liberty to offer it

11

to me realizing that I was left in the cold by myself with nowhere to go. I thanked him and offered to pay for the room. He refused to take my money. I realized that it was a sympathetic kindness that he was doing for a lost stranger. I crawled into bed under the blanket not having taken my clothes off for more warmth, and slept until around five o'clock in the morning. I got up, brushed my teeth, picked up my suitcase and left. I started wandering the neighborhood hoping that somehow the situation would resolve itself. How? I did not really know. I could not reach Micheline since I did not have a phone number where I could reach her. I was growing a bit desperate. I was tired, hungry and felt lost. I walked around and around until a car stopped and it was Micheline who was there inviting me over. She then explained that she had been to the train station with her friend, Ben, at the time I had given her for the incoming train. But I had not taken that one. I had taken a later train and she did not know that. I had tried reaching her at her residence but no one answered. She had moved by then and I did not know that. So she decided to roam the neighborhood streets thinking I would be there if I had arrived the night before. It was indeed a wise action on her part. Good thinking. I hopped into the car and off we went to the friends's house in Nice. What a relief, I told myself. Micheline was all smiles and started to explain things to me. That she had to move out of the little house due to a hurtful experience she had with one of the ladies who owned the place. The lady had accused her of not being friendly enough and even blamed her for the coldness of the rapport that had developed between Micheline and her. The lady got very nervous and even mad and had hit Micheline. Micheline was in tears. The other lady, the sister, tried to reconcile or mend the situation, but Micheline told her she and her children could no longer live there. That's when she called her friends who offered her their home until she could find some place to stay. That was the story I got from Micheline. I felt bad for her and I did not know if I should stay or not. She told me that her friends wanted me to stay with them and the Bousquet family. I found them very sympa as they say in France. They would be gone for the day as they were working in Monaco. I would be on my own but I did not mind that. I would roam the streets of Nice and visit the shops. The girls would be at school. I shared the meals with them and I would bring "home" some offering that I purchased on

12

the way back from town. It was my contribution in some way. One day I found out it was Ben's birthday, so I purchased a birthday cake for him. He was delighted. We all were. It became a festive occasion for all of us. I truly felt at home. Micheline tried very hard to make me feel that way.

On a bright sunny weekend afternoon, I asked Micheline if I could interview her and get her thoughts on painting and her artistic philosophy. She agreed to do so. These are her thoughts on her art. She answered all my questions and even elaborated on several. The first question was on her works of art and her philosophy of art. She answered by saying quite forcefully and precisely that she had no philosophy as such except that her philosophy was her own experiences put into action. She painted what she felt and experienced in life. She did not adhere to a movement nor to any set of rules. She did not follow the classical style nor the very popular Impressionism although she somewhat admired certain artists such as Cézanne and Van Gogh. She much preferred contemporary artists, someone like Kadinski, Jackson Pollack, and Frank Stella.

The interview started by my simply asking her to talk to me about her art, the practice of her art as well as her philosophy of art if she had one. Her first response was, "First of all I have some ideas that are quite precise on art, on my art in particular and also how I conceive the activity that one would call art that for me equals creativity." She went on to say, "One of the criteria that I use when I'm doing my work is that I must have the possibility of creating something that was non-existent beforehand. It has to be without any exterior support from the point of view that I cannot look at a landscape and try to reproduce this landscape even at the impressionist level, but rather transform this landscape perhaps some sensations that I would have from a landscape and try to capture the sensations."

I followed up on her response by telling her that her work of art was not impressionist but is based on reproduced sensations. She answered, "Yes, reproduced sensations while…each one of us understands that we could look at a landscape and we would have a different in-

13

terpretation or a different sensation. And when it comes to a visual image, because I do watercolors, that visual image must not only capture simply the sensations that I have and translate them into a visual form, in a visual image that honestly reproduces my sensations not to please others, not to please commercially, but must be truly my experience with this support. However, with most of my art work, I do not work with exterior support, but rather an imaginary support. What does that mean? I start to work without any vision. Most of my work, I would say ninety-five percent is done that way. I begin with taches[spots] of color, with those taches one tache brings another and there are forms that begin to develop, textures that play with the paper that come out of the paper and I try to enter into harmony with the work that unfolds before me. And often during a work I can think that, ah, now I have found it and I want to take a certain direction and in the middle of the road change completely."

I then asked her if she took her art from experience, sensations even feelings. She said, "Feelings, yes. Feelings for me mean that I know all the things that I live in life be they joyous, gay, or sad, and those are sooner or later translated into a painting." I then stated that she would say that her art was subjective rather than objective, rather based on sensations, feelings than on the intelligence which is cerebral. She answered, " No," and she started to chuckle. I then told her to explain.

Her explanation was, "First of all, there are sensations, but I believe that the intellectual side, the cerebral side enters, comes into it. Let's say I begin a painting with sensations, but in order to finish there must be a cerebral exercise that takes place. For me, it cannot simply be a mixture of colors. The cerebral exercise enters when I look at a form that unfolds before my eyes and I try at that very moment to render it a little more concrete. There is an enormous equilibrium or I try to get an equilibrium between what is being said and what is not said in the painting, and that's where it becomes not simply... it no longer remains at the feeling level, but one must attain a certain cerebral capacity."

I then asked if this did not touch upon symbolism. Her answer: "Yes, but it's a symbolism that is mine which is personal, altogether personal." I then told her that her work had to be profoundly personal. "Yes, yes," she exclaimed. " I could not describe it otherwise."

As a follow-up, I asked her, "You told me once that Madame Ro-che(one of the two ladies who let her have a small residence in Saint-Jean-Cap-Ferrat) insisted that you drew your inspiration from your intestines, 'from your guts' and it mounted to the cerebration up in the head and came out through the way of the tactile sensations or out of your fingers, your hands. Is that true? Is it still the avenue of your art?"
Her answer, "I think that Madame Roche was one of the first persons who had the possibility of explaining with words what I was doing. And I was comfortable with her manner of seeing things. I believe that what I do is truly a thought, but it's a thought that comes from the tripes[intestines], . but it must pass through the head and come out of at the fingertips. It simply cannot be painting in which, let's say, a painting where I would me defoulerais/work off my tensions completely as well as my feelings. There is a moment when the work of art can begin like that, but it must finish much more structured for me." I replied that if that were the case it would risk becoming also sentimental. She answered, "Yes."

I then asked her where did she get her inspiration, and she replied "Honestly tell you where my inspiration comes from?" And I said, "How does inspiration work for you? When do you feel inspired? When you sit down, you sit there then you tell yourself today I begin because it's time." She answered, "Oh, I feel it. It's on account of a level of sensations. If too many days go by without doing some painting, without trying to make something, there is a tension that is being built and it's a tension that I cannot live with for too long. I must absolutely work." I told her that her work then becomes almost a catharsis because she feels the stress, the need to release what is in "your tripes, your intestines, let's say." And she quickly replied, "Oui, oui." I then added that it was not an inspiration out of a clear blue sky. "You sit down and voilà." I then asked her to describe the process, the inspiration and a work of art.

She said, "Okay. You take a painting, a very specific painting, the painting of Chernobyl. Okay? And you're going to get a slide of that(I never did get one), the painting of Chernobyl was inspired by a specific event, precise, that upset me very very much and made me feel that we were truly absolutely impotent in front of life's events at this actual moment and that in spite of a whole raised conscience to not want to proliferate in nuclear arms, not to do things with the nuclear, with all the opposition, there was nothing to do. That we were in the nuclear age, that we were not going to get out of it, and that left me with an enormous despair. The reality of being truly and totally powerless, me..ah, I don't believe too much in paintings that are political. I do not look to express myself in that fashion, but I know that the Chernobyl painting started to emerge by its sensations of powerlessness and when I began to work on the painting, I started with the three mushrooms of color which for me were like explosions. And after having placed these three explosions on the sheet, I had to finish it. I had to establish a balance, a harmony in the composition. And that's when I placed very geometric forms, very solid that could symbolize… ah, the buildings that were exploding, but rather it was in the choices of colors and not simply forms. The colors are very heavy, they're not gay." "So colors for you produce a certain effect but also they have a certain symbol or colors that mean such and such," I added. "Yes, but I did not learn what the colors meant to say," she said. "I know that each color has a symbolism and there are even studies based on the symbolism of colors." "When you use the red color for you, it's a certain symbol, when you use blue or the green or paler colors and…" "Yes," she added, "I don't think blue equals sky." "Agreed." I added, "Or red equals fire." "Not at all," she replied. And then I said, "But rather a feeling, a presentiment? Or a reaction?" "Yes, if I try to express myself or express something, it's this mixture of colors, ah…" "So you think in colors." "Yes, which is very strong in me. Ah, but it's not uniquely in symbolism that we have learned, and for me in a certain way throughout my studies of colors, it's rather arbitrary." "Nothing pre-established," I said. "No, nothing. I would not put black simply because it's somber, and that one should have a morbid reaction in front of the black. I would not put red to make a painting explode. I do not think that way. If red is convenient with the other colors that were already put in if it can give me what I want or what I feel I want, I will go with red."

I then told her that she was touching upon what I had called before this harmony, this agencement of colors of hers. And I added that was why I recognized something different artistically speaking. Then I asked her to speak about this agencement, this harmony of colors. "The harmony of colors," she told me, "is completely innate. I believe that it's the part, if one can speak of gifts, for me it's a part of myself that is natural. I know that those colors are in harmony, but I cannot give a cerebral reason why. I know it, I feel it, you can see it." She added that it happened for each work. Each work received the same amount of..." "So," I said, "the colors for a watercolor are different from the colors for an oil painting, for a pastel, right?" She answered, "Yes." I then asked her why she had chosen the watercolor as medium. She went on to explain why. "First of all, it's the sense of fluidity. I also chose it because at the very beginning I had heard that it was the most difficult medium to control, to master and that was a normal challenge for me. What was the most difficult. I could not see myself in oils although I had done oils and one day I will perhaps do some again, but for me watercolors allow me an enormous amount of versatility, of flexibility, that I find very very important in my art work, although the idea that watercolor is flexible, it is not. That's the way it is for me. However, I like the fact that it is mixed with water and not turpentine or something else. I like the sensation of water. And, when one works on a watercolor, when it's trempé/ watered or we work on a wet sheet, there's always a color there....but when it dries it becomes something else. You must know what it will become. You must know the pigments because pigments react differently when they dry. There are some that polarize themselves. Thus, it gives me the sensation of being grainy that can be agencé/organized in a composition to render the work much more interesting." " So, the color on you palette is never the color that will be reproduced, let's say, in the same fashion." "No." "Mixed with water and put on the paper, because the paper is always different." " Yes, although I work uniquely with two different papers." Then I asked her, "What kind of paper do you use?"

"I work most of the time with the Arche that is very well known, but there is another French paper that I like as much and it's the Lana which is a paper that.....there is almost a kind of sweetness in the way it absorbs, for me, the water and the pigment. There is a reaction a little bit different, one could say that the Arche is a little stiffer while Lana , for me, is more supple. And the works that have a tendency of being very fluid, less structured, are usually more of a success on the Lana. The paper is very important." I followed with, "You spoke of a challenge. Isn't it true that when you have both the color and the water, it's very fluid, it flows, that you could pour very easily…Perhaps according to me, aren't you afraid of sometimes of couler/running… that it will create spots…What do you do then? Can you erase that? Can you?" " We can erase but if there is a blot, my first reaction is not to erase. If there is a blot that is present, that I did not want, instead of having it as an error, I incorporate it naturally in the work and I work with it." "It's like hazard that presented itself." " Yes, yes, yes…and then the challenge arrives because it's not funny to spoil at the last moment and have the necessity to change." "Is it possible to erase certain colors once placed there?" "Yes, yes, absolutely…I have to divulge my secret." And she laughed. I answered, "I do not know if it's a secret or a style…but you told me that no one can reproduce what you do, so you can teach everything that you know but they can never become another Bousquet."

"No, no, it's true, it's true. It's very easy, it depends." "Are you the only one that employs that moyen/means?" " Oh, no, I'm sure that it's used elsewhere." "A toothbrush, right?" "It is a toothbrush. We can do it with a sponge, but the support, to erase the support is very very important. With the paper Arche and the paper Lana we can erase with a toothbrush, rewet the paper and remove most of all the pigments except a few that are pigments that stain and cannot be removed easily at all. There's always a little that stays. But it's the paper that renders that possibility." "Are watercolors always done on white paper, never on colored paper?" "Yes, they can be done on colored paper but at that moment it's paper that must be treated in a certain way to receive…in order to be a good support for the watercolor because there are problems that take place after oxidation. And the work, after all, must have the capacity of a certain permanence." "You once said that you had never taken an art course and that your art truly came from your talents. You want to talk about your debut in art?"

"Yes. The debuts are very personal. The start came in 1968, no, in 1978-1979. I was a student at the University of Massachusetts. I was working on a masters. I was very interested in children and their capacity to create. I was working with handicapped children. I was working with daycare centers and nursery schools at the University, but I was not terribly happy. I had gone through a divorce. I had two young children, really young, one still in diapers, where I spent a dirty moment in my life. One day, a friend of mine came to see me and gave me tubes of acrylics, some canvases, and brushes telling me that it will do you some good, a little, and perhaps there is something there to express. Well, I did not take her advice. I did nothing for a month, six weeks. One night I woke up in the middle of the night. I felt panicky. I felt truly bad. I did not know what to do anymore and I started to paint, like that. The hours passed. The day started and for one reason or another, there was something with this action of painting that had been dislodged in me." "Was it truly the first time that you put paint, color on paper?" "It was probably the first time, except when I was very very young around fourteen years old, fifteen, even younger, I remember I truly loved to color. But I hated to color in coloring books. I did not like the lines. I did not like a drawing already made for me. And, often everything that was given to me as gifts and everything my parents bought me or my mother bought me were coloring books" Laughter.

"Coloring books?" "Yes, coloring books. But I adored working. And I will ever remember working with the first crayolas in my life. I still love crayolas." Laughter. "And after this episode, what was the development of art for you?" "I continued to work totally like an exercise….exutoire/release. Completely. I continued my studies besides and I spent some time in Italy. I came back from Italy totally mixed up[bouleversée] because I had discovered again another culture, another way of life, so I started to paint a lot. And one day, ah, let's say, one of the fine arts professors discovered that I was doing some art work and he was very moved by what I was doing. He told me there was something there and that I was wasting my time in administration or in pursuing courses in human development, and that I should probably do something creatively from the viewpoint of painting. He offered me an exhibition at the university. That's how I got started." "It was in oils not in watercolors, I believe." "It was in acrylics… yes, and in Indian ink/encre de Chine also. I had done some drawings in Indian ink. So, little by little it was like a snowball and one day I put in my head that is what I wanted to do." "You never took a course in drawing." "I took a course in drawing that lasted half a semester out of which I got the commentary from the woman teacher, 'Better to go elsewhere.' Laughter. "Why? Because..." "Because I did not succeed in doing what she wanted me to do. I always did according to my stubborn head and I was a perturbing element in class." "After that you did not take any other lessons?" "No, no, no, no. I was completely discouraged." Laughter. "Because you did not like to follow the rules of others in a given way?"

Micheline continued on this subject. "No. It's true that I do not like to follow the regulations of others simply to follow them . I never was like that. It's not in my personality. But I never understood why one could not cohabitate...ah...and have a reason for these rules and try to go beyond rules, go beyond the limits imposed arbitrarily. For me all rules and regulations are always arbitrary. It doesn't mean that I don't see the necessity of rules. I believe that in never having done the fine arts, I Imposed on myself some rules much harder these last few years. Even now since I work a lot. Normally I work not less than ten hours per day and that's not ten hours of creativity when I turn out a painting...ah...which is a success but rather in searching for rules." "Personal?" "Personal." "For your art?" "Yes, there are some."

I asked her, "When did you begin the watercolors?" "In 1982 because I was too poor to buy oils." "So, necessity forced you to take another medium." "Yes." " Which in a certain fashion truly found its launching, its blossoming." "Yes, it was that in combination with the fact that someone had told me that it was the most difficult medium to master." " So as a rebel you felt that..." "Yes, because it was another rule that someone..." Laughter. "I want to show them." " Yes. Be it a good thing to be hardheaded or not, I do not know."

I continued by asking her about her displacement to Europe. "Your art began, let's say, at the university. Now it developed in Europe. Why did you choose France?" "Because my name is Micheline Bousquet and because I am up to my neck of living in a country that could not pronounce my name. Canada was too cold, so frankly there was only France on the European continent, Belgium was not possible." "You already had come to Italy." "Yes, I had come to Italy before. I knew that I wanted to be on the continent of Europe." "You did not think that in a North-American milieu you could create as well as in Europe?" " No. Not because it was North-America but it was because I had lived and started a whole life that is completely different from what I have now. And I needed to do a divorce with that and the divorce meant for me make a culture die or a way of life in order to adopt and adapt myself to a new one." " This change, this modification, was especially for a rupture rather than an artistic élan?" "I believe that it was for a rupture. I believe also that I had well understood that tension, the unknown, the fear can probably be utilized as a motivating factor in creativity. And I knew that in disembarking in a country that I did not know at all, that I knew no one, that I would be pushed to my limits."

I retorted by saying, " You had chosen France because you spoke French? You did not choose Italy nor Spain nor Germany." "No." "It's a factor." "It's a factor." "Cultural." "It's a cultural factor. Yes." "Perhaps profoundly Franco-American, Francophone, bilingual." "Yes. And I believe in a certain way that I had the necessity to return, let's say, to my roots, to see what it was to try to understand, to go full circle in some way."[she used the idiom boucler la boucle which is not used ordinarily by Francos. This to show that she had already adapted quite well]. "The ancestors who come from France, emigrated to Quebec, then New England, and I believe that I come full circle. It's important to me."

"Why did you select the Midi de la France rather than, let's say, Paris?" "Because I had…ah…there are many reasons. One of the first reasons was because it was so very close to where the Impressionists had done their work there. I was a bit seduced by that fact. I was seduced again by the fact that there was a light that I had heard of." "But, the Impressionists, in great majority did their work very close to Paris." "Yes, but they did a lot here." "Some like Renoir." "And Cézanne…Van Gogh." "Cézanne and Van Gogh were not true Impressionists but rather post-Impressionists, they say. So they were like the bridge between the two. Truly you followed in their footsteps but it was especially the light that you wanted to capture."

"And I think that I was probably afraid of going to Paris right away, you know. I saw the Midi like a little slower, a little easier to accéder/ attain." "A little warmer also." Laughter. "Yes." "Paris of your evolution. You started in '81,'82 the watercolor. That's already four years. There was certainly an evolution from '82 to '86." "Okay. Since '82 I have not worked uniquely with watercolors. I worked with watercolors until mid '83. After that I worked a lot with oils, then I worked with oils up until , let's say, the end of '83. So watercolors are still very young for me. But since '86 I've been working uniquely with it and a lot, a lot, a lot...so the evolution came very rapidly. It's because I feel comfortable in that medium. I never felt comfortable in anything else.." "What have you learned since the beginning?" "What do you mean what have I learned?" "With your watercolors you certainly learned certain techniques, certain things." "Yes. At the beginning it was rather, let's say, watercolor with...I did have such... ah...a large range of colors. What does it mean. It means the intensity of colors. I was always with middle values although the substance of my watercolors there was probably always an ethereal sensation that was of other dimensions...that was truly original. The fact of developing technically, I arrived in expressing with greater success through a larger gamut of the value of colors." "What do you mean by the value of colors?" "Value is the intensity of colors, from the darker to the much lighter and know how to oppose them in a work." "In the beginning you had less of this gamut." "Yes." "Today you have more of this gamut." "Yes." "You have more of this agencement/harmony of different colors, pale and stronger and less strong." "Yes. And I understand a lot more now ..ah...the juxtaposition of colors. What can one color bring to another. The harmony that takes place. Not simply in what one calls the complementary colors but the mixtures that happen totally...ah...au pif/at random. For me because the palette is continually very dirty. I do not try to clean it and I never work with one color by itself. By that I mean a pure color. I will always put the brush in one color and after that right away I will put it in another godet/pot and I mix the colors."

"I noticed that your brushes are not artist brushes. They're brushes that wall painters could also use." Laughter. " Yes." "In your case is it unique or probably it's a stereotype that I'm making?" " I think that it's probably a stereotype that you make because those brushes that you saw me working with come from the United-States. They are not accessible in France." Laughter. "They're very wide." "Yes. And there's some much larger. But their price is prohibitive because I still have one that's larger than that." "What kind of hair do you use?" "That's synthetic hair. It's a synthetic that was made…ah…that has a longevity of…frankly…I will never have to rebuy that brush if I take good care of it. It's a synthetic that gives the brush an enormous suppleness which is very very important. It's very light and it was very very well conceived." "How many different brushes do you use in one watercolor?" "Not more than five." "Five." "Yes. Max." "Probably one. Maybe." "There's always two that I work with. For the finish work at that very moment work with three others that make things completely different."

" The other tool also is the hair dryer because I saw you…" " I use the hair dryer and that's magnifique. It's a tool that I discovered recently. If you have enough water on the paper with pigment with the air from the hair dryer you can push into forms and textures, create unique textures that you cannot do with a brush. I use table salt to make special effects. I use anything I can think of to make special effects." "I've seen that you use cut-outs, no? "Yes. Yes…ah…often when I want to lighten or give a movement to a certain part of a work that is not there, that is already very colored, at that moment I do cut-outs in the form that I want and I take out with a toothbrush the color in the shape of the cut-outs. For me everything is permitted…ah…except that it can never become a gimmick." "It's not copying." " No. We must not find in each work the same utilization, the same way of…these accessories. For me at that moment it becomes something that…is more authentic but a repetition. And if I based my thoughts on the fact that I I must create something inexistent beforehand. ..ah…I abhor that one can look at one of my art works and say, they're all the same. I want each one to be different." "I perceive also in the evolution that there is a certain structure, so I would like to talk about structure. At the beginning, there was a certain structure often very delineated because there was the structure of the woman especially. I never saw a work of a man." "No." "I never mentioned that. But it was always the woman. And more structured with geometry sometimes, structured in a symbolist way, structured a lot in…ah…a kind of art much more contemporary, if you want, and I say that because we had discussed this work… ah…that I have because we asked ourselves what name should we give it. I had suggested Crystaline, Crystalization, and I saw at the vernissage/ opening reception that it was Structures. You told me that it was an important work of art because it was that one that made in a way the bridge between the old and the new. You want to talk about that?" (Big sigh) "Yes. Where to begin? First of all I recognize that I started sooner to do painting especially watercolors with characters to be repeated. Probably what was it that I saw, things that were more concrete. There was a development and I believe that it was a development of maturity towards something much more abstract. I don't think I can come back on women although at a certain era I had wanted to do a series of works on women. If I do it, it will be done in a very different way. Up to now, I do not want the figuration. In order to make the change of women, characters, where I am right now, I believe that I had to go through a moment of a lot of fluidity in my art that was much less structured than it is at this moment. To make pigments flow, to agencer/harmonize in a way that renders a form comprehensible enough, but still fluid. And I need finally to push the technique, I believe. the watercolor. To structure, work to a level that needs to be worked. You must work at it, you must work at it up to the point where I tell myself not another mark because it would be too worked up. In watercolors one can easily work it up too much."

I then asked, "Would you say that the blossoming forth of your abstract art now much more abstract and structured, is a blossoming of symbolism for you?" "What do you mean by that?" "An effort to render the structure more symbolist?" "With what goal in mind?" "I don't know since you had fluidity before. It seems to me there was less structure less…not necessarily framework but less geometry less lines and less colors." "But I had less experience with the technique." "So, it's really the elaboration of the technique." "Maybe we cannot separate between technique, maturity, evolution, and all of that. You understand what I want to say?" "Yes,"I replied. Micheline then said, "I'm not sure that I can compartmentalize like that since I arrive at being better in the technique, better in expressing myself." "More complex is your work." "Yes, yes, yes." "Where is Micheline Bousquet's art going? It's now '86 and we're approaching '87. Where is her art going? What is the future development? What would you want to realize?" "Well, for sure I'm convinced that I have not yet stunned the world. That I am far from expressing myself as much as I need to. Probably it will never come. But I am far very very far from being satisfied. I would like to work from the point of view of format if we are speaking of technique. I would like to have the capacity of working on a much larger format, to have greater space, to say things. I know that I have limits but I don't know where they are and because I do not know where they are, I do not feel these limits. I would love simply to have the possibility of going as far as I can." "You say that you have not yet touched the apex and that it's going to develop more and more and so it's a challenge for you of always discover, rediscover and have, let's say, probably a new technique, a new orientation. More and more maturity and technique in your art are developing, so you do not know exactly where your art will go." "No." "But you know that it's going in more complex direction." "I feel it." "You sense it." "And I see it." "Now, you are in the process of contemplating a displacement towards Paris. What does that mean in your art?" "First of all, it signifies an enormous possibility of going much further…ah…without a doubt Paris has a stimulation that I could not find here on the Côte d'Azur. It has a structure in itself of art that is much more cosmopolitan, more sophisticated. We cannot deny that. There's the contact with other cities in Europe, other cities in the U.S. that is made much more easily. An exchange that can take place much easier. Maybe more sensitive. Much more ready to receive Micheline Bousquets. But it scares me because I know also that there will be much more competition."

"Does Paris mean for you an artistic development? A possibility of contacts in order to learn or especially the possibility of making contact for other vernissages/openings and what Parisians and the French call following the English, marketing?" "No. First of all, for me Paris it's the possibility of placing myself in an environment that I do not know. Once more, it's a challenge to see what that can bring me. And it's not simply at the artistic level but at the personal level. And the artistic level reflects also the personal level. They're tied together. They're never detached. I hope that Paris will open up for me horizons and that it will be reflected in my art. Now, it's evident that on the marketing level there are many more possible openings. But it's not solely for that." "I understand, but like the Impressionists you certainly feel the obligation to support yourself, your family, so it's very difficult often with a lack of money. When you are not always at ease. Does that bouleverse/bowl you over? Sometimes? Are you not often in insecurity and then you tell yourself what am I doing? Should I continue? Or..." "Yes, often." Laughter. "Not simply the possibility. It's the reality of things." It's the reality of things and quite often there are doubts, and quite often I ask myself questions. There was always something that happened very little after that eliminated the doubt. Be it that I sold a painting, be it...there is another possibility of continuing to move. That's an acheminement/forwarding of art in life. The door has never been closed up until that moment, and I believe that I can be in the material security or even emotional, to self-doubt. There was always someone, something, an event...that allowed me to continue." " So, the development of your art will happen in Paris. You are going probably make contact with other cities." " Yes." "But most probably in the future the two great centers will be Paris and Montreal." "Yes. Which pleases me very much, first of all." "That will truly make the bilan/balance between Franco-American culture and Europe." "Yes, yes." "Do you believe that your Francophone reality, your Franco-American heritage helps you, hurts you or is not significant in your artistic development?" " That it's not significant?" "I'm asking you the question. Is it or not? Is it getting in your way or do you think it's hurting you? Do you think that it adds something or it does nothing one way or another?" "Oh, no, It's not indifferent. I believe there are parts that harm and I believe that there are parts that help me a lot. Parts that do harm are often values with which we were rather raised as women. Always those questionings on the way or the way in which I am a mother because I have two children. The children who must come before me...ah....how we make sacrifices, and that we must always make some in order to be successful. And I do not believe in it. I believe the idea of putting self modestly in life without ever saying, I am and I am very good in what I do,, and have difficulties in telling self, to be, and to pursue because we have obligations elsewhere…ah…which is not career, that cannot ever be the egocentric expression of everything that art represents. ..ah, no, no… I think it was difficult enough, it remains always a little difficult to take the first step and make decisions that are for the advancement of my art. Of myself because myself and my art that's the same thing. I live my art. I am my art. It's not…there's no separation for me. But it took me a very very long time to arrive at that thought. To not arrive at that thought but to accept this way of being. There are things I believe that in our culture, the way we were brought up that can do harm. But there are also sides…ah…I believe if I did not have those doubts, do not forget that doubts bring tensions, and for me tension equals creativity. So, there is a sensibility, and I believe that everything I do in my art is due to the necessity to express, express myself and give me permission to express myself. But, I believe that it's an art that is sensitive and that sensitivity comes truly from my childhood experiences, from culture. I never felt good in my being[se sentir bien dans sa peau], neither in Canada nor in the U.S. I was the canayenne and the canuck. I never found where I could hang my hat." Forced laughter. "To really feel good. All this for me enters in all that I do now. It's an all." "So, it's almost a discovery of your identity, cultural and artistic." "Yes, yes," in a low and subdued voice.

"I have many dreams. The artistic dream…well I do have an artistic dream perhaps very down to earth and perhaps also very much tied to a disguised Francophone culture. I want to leave something of myself, not simply to my children, but that will have the name Bousquet. I want people to know that one can create as well, one can have something to offer." "You mentioned several times the name Bousquet, so you are quite proud of your name." "Finally." "French and Franco-American." "Finally. It took me several years." "Really?" "Oh yes. I hated the price of Micheline for a very long time. No one could pronounce it." "Because often as a Franco-American we try to become Yankee or American." "Even my parents do not call me Micheline." "Really." "They call me Mikeline." Laughter. "Once in a while my father calls me Micheline." "Yet, they're the ones who gave you this French name." "Yes, yes." "Model. Do you have an artistic model in life?" "There are many." "Heroes or heroines?" "First of all, from the point of view of technique…truth be told, I feel very very small and

I will always be very small in spite that the evolution of my technique can evolve again, again, again. I hope exponentially, but it's Turner. To think what Turner has done in 1835 and at that era, it's phenomenal. The old man/bonhomme was a genius...of watercolor. Now I really like contemporary artists...ah, I could truly appreciate Jackson Pollack. People who dare...I do not say , I cannot always be in agreement with the result...their work... probably it does not please me but the fact that they dare...ah.... inspires me. Tells me that everything is possible. It lets me dream." Then I asked her, "You spoke of the Impressionists. Is there an Impressionist that inspires you more than others?" "Probably not an Impressionist but a Post-Impressionist who was Van Gogh. As much for his works as his life. I never had a problem in understanding why he had cut off his ear. It never made me nuts about it. It was normal, natural." "For him." "For him." "Finally, you have already mentioned that you give courses." "Oh, yes." "Moreover, you go out among the people with the technique and the art. That art is not something in a studio...or the snob...or something closed in. Do you want to talk to me about that?" "Yes. First of all, I believe profoundly that we all have the need to create. Especially at this time the creativity of long ago simply around the house or, let's say, our ancestors even in Canada who were on the farm and who had so much work to do. They had to direct their activity to their problems. At this time, a lot of our activity is purely cerebral. We do not have this sensation of working from our tripes/guts and have a tangible product and that truly reflects us. And for me to take my work on the streets or to put it in public and talk about what I do, how I do it, why I do it is part of my responsibility, I believe. I believe there is a gift, I think there are innate things and certainly agencements/harmonies of colors, a harmony that I can bring to bear on a painting...I have this capacity of expressing oneself much more easily than maybe someone next to me. But I recognize that the person next to me has as much need if he knows it or not, if he admits it or not, to express himself, and consequently it's not enough for me to simply bring my works to the public, try to sell them, to commercialize them...ah...no, we must share this capacity hoping that even if someone cannot redo a Micheline Bousquet he will be able to find a way of ...défouler/releasing, of expressing, of creating also themselves even if it remains always in the family...ah...try...one day. I have someone who surpasses me, so much the better...I succeeded. It's a one hundred percent success."

I then asked her, "What do you want to give or leave to your students? Fundamentally." "Stop being afraid...of their imagination." "If I understand you well, you do not teach so much art or even a technique, you teach them how to discover themselves their own talents, their own technique." "Yes, yes. And because I do it well with watercolors, I have to use the watercolor as a tool. It's a tool for me. I could not teach them, for example, the same thing through oils because I cannot do oils as I do watercolor or pastels. Maybe one day, but not now." "Well, do you have something to add? In French or in English?" "I know this interview has gone on..." "Now say everything you said in French in English now," "No, no, no, no." Laugher. "You'll have to get it translated, Norman." Long pause. "I suppose...what I'd like to say, what I'd like to convey to whoever listens or however this tape is utilized later on, that I think that people really, really need to accept within themselves...and recognize first of all within themselves the need to create. It doesn't have to be a painting. It can be music. It can be...ah...wood sculptures. It can be paper dolls...But that they will give themselves permission to do this without saying I can't do it or it's horrible. And that they will persist in trying to continue exploring themselves through a creativity, through an act of creativity. Whatever one fears, whatever one...no I guess what I really want to say and I'm struggling to say it, dare to dream. Simply dare to dream and believe in that dream. And go after it. That' it."

As I have said, this interview took place in Nice on December 11, 1986, in Micheline Bousquet's friends's apartment. Ben and Janine. I forget their last names, but it's not really important. It was right after lunch that we went into the bedroom, closed the door, sat down and began to talk. The friends were away at work in Monaco while the two girls were playing in the living room. I wanted to make sure that we would have the only quiet space available that afternoon for I considered this interview as an important part of my sabbatical research project. I had a small tape recorder with which I wanted to record the interview for future use as a document and possible essay or novel. I wasn't yet determined what I was going to do with it. It would sit in my desk drawer for quite a while, even years, since there was no pressure to do anything with it then. I did not have to report it to the Dean nor to the chair of the Humanities. I was chair of the department of the Humanities anyway. The tape would serve as a testimony of one of my research endeavors. I was doing it since it was a good link with the cultural part of my sabbatical which was linking France, Quebec and New England Francophone French cultural dimensions of the three areas where ancestral ties had been established over the years. These ties were part of Micheline Bousquet's life as well as mine. We were both what was called Franco-American. This term is applied to people of French ancestry whose maternal language is French and who live usually in some part of New England. We are dealing here with a fairly large population and it's the largest ethnic group of Maine where Micheline and I grew up.

Well, as a published author, I realize that the very beginning of this work is rather an unusual start for a biography. It's not a novel, one that merges together action, adventure, different people, and geography to make it flow and bring in the reader to expect more. No, it's a dialogue between two friends who discuss art and the kind of philosophy of art that is, at times, somewhat boring to some readers. It's certainly not a Charles Dickens novel nor a John Grisham reader with adventurous and thrilling happenings. I'll admit that the translation of an interview that was done thirty-five years ago is not what to expect from an author who claims to be writing a novel or any written work. But, you see this work is an analytical biography where I try to analyze the core of what exactly is creative art as done by one artist. Creativity is the core here. It may be dull to some but for me and to those who enjoy such literature, it becomes a story, the story of a life in action, artistic action that was Micheline Bousquet's. I waited until I had let this project stew in my mind and felt ready to put it down in writing. Besides it was time to write about Micheline Bousquet. I did not know if she was still alive or not. Oh, God. I was somewhat in a dilemma. To write or not to write. In my mind, I was afraid that if I started writing Micheline's biography, I would probably have to face the reality of her death. I did not want to do that. I did not want her to pass away. I did not want her to die. That would mean that I would lose a friend. A very close friend. There were so many things that I still wanted to tell her, so many chances that I had not yet taken to be with her, face to face, and just talk like friends do. However, I knew in my creative mind and my author's heart that someday I would have to start writing about the superb and troubled artist that I got to know and admire, Micheline Bousquet. I simply hoped and prayed for my friend's survival from the many challenges she had to face day to day. Since I had not heard from her for such a long time, I began to worry..and probably despair. I just had to sit down and write even though I wasn't sure I could. I wasn't certain that I could write well enough about someone who most probably had disappeared from my life. I just wanted to do her justice. I so wanted to find the words that would express her life and her achievements in daring creativity. So, one day I did sit down and started to write with one of her small oil paintings that she had given me the last time I sat with her in Varengeville-sur-mer. Talk about inspiration.

People often ask me where do I get my inspiration for my books. I've written twenty-seven books so far, about half of them are in French. I get it from many sources, from my own experiences and travels, stories that I have read, incidents that were related to me and other sources. One such source is my travel to Paris for a summer seminar under the guidance of Professor Murray of Columbia University to study Gothic architecture in the Île-de-France in 1989. Having experienced the marvel of Gothic architecture and its various cathedrals such as Notre-Dame de Chartres and Notre-Dame d'Amiens, I decided to write my own story of an architect who goes through the various steps of the architecture guild to become a master builder and build his own cathedral. I had the many components of gothic cathedral building having spent time climbing the rooftops of cathedrals and experiencing the Gothic space of interiors as well as listening to Professor Murray explaining the height of particular pillars in a given cathedral. Enough to be able to write a novel about it. The culmination was the publication of my book, Cajetan the Stargazer.

I decided to write this particular analytical biography, as I call it, when I realized that I was good at writing novels that dealt with artists that I found fascinating. My first such work was on Van Gogh, The Boy With the Blue Cap---Van Gogh in Arles. Then I wrote one on Émile Friant, The Man With the Easel of Horn---Émile Friant. I had seen his painting La Douleur in a film, "Il y a longtemps que je t'aime" and was deeply inspired to do research on him and write a novel about a not too well-known artist. Then I wanted to write one about a woman artist and I chose Rosa Bonheur, the woman who had to ask permission from the police to wear pants in public, The Day the Horses Went to the Fair---Animal Lover Rosa Bonheur. What inspired me was her huge painting at the Metropolitan Museum of Art in New York in front of which I stood there a long time gazing at this marvelous rendition of draft horses. So, this is my attempt to write about a woman who adored the art of watercolors then oil paintings and principally her passion for creativity. Creativity lends itself well to analysis rather than concrete manifestations of fine arts alone. The two go well together. That's what I intend to do with my experiences, with my artist friend and the many notes taken over the years as well as the many letters that I received from her as well as a number of emails. I will gather all this information and analyze it in a way as to reveal to the reader who Micheline Bousquet was and what she did and how she thought about art and creativity. She was truly a daring person and a daring artist. Above all, I knew her as a courageous and caring woman. Most of all, she knew how to read your mind and heart so that she could introspectively assess your talents and your weaknesses. She had her finger on your pulse and she could tell you just what ailed you without judging you. I came to know her inside out and considered her to be an honest, vulnerable at times, and sincere friend. Besides she was Une bonnefemme aux aguets de l'évolution de la femme. A dame ever on the lookout for the feminine evolution, I would say.

Micheline Bousquet was born in 1946 in Lewiston, Maine of middle-class parents, the father, a family doctor and the mother a conservative and proud woman who had learned to play the violin but hid her instrument under the cover of the living room furniture. She would not acquiesce her talents as a musician but rather hid it under the proverbial bushel basket. Why? No one seemed to know. She was a haughty, introverted and difficult person to understand who had to have her own way all the time. Micheline always suffered under her mother's tutelage. She could never understand her mother's wishes and dealings, especially her mother's lack of true and sincere affection.

The Bousquets raised three children, one son and two daughters. All three went to parochial schools and were raised with the ethnic values of duty and religious fervor. Both parents valued the sophistication of position in society. Both parents appreciated the marked good behavior on the part of their children. They were all expected to behave like young grown-ups, as one would say. You just did not show excitement and strong desires for things. "Fais pas ton excitée"/don't get wild was the dictate and rule of the day of the mother to her daughter, Micheline. Micheline apparently was a vigorous and happy child who got excited over almost anything. Her mother had a hard time tolerating this. She wanted her daughter to behave well and be a good child in front of others especially company. In some way, she even considered Micheline a rebel and a disobedient individual. She tried over and over again to reform her and give her the right set of rules that she, the mother, had learned and adopted as a woman of class. She thought she had married class by marrying her husband, Jean, a respected physician of the community. She became the proper wife of the proper husband. She expected her children to behave properly all the time.

When Micheline could not and would not obey the strict rules of both society and parental guidance, she was sent away to school in or around Montreal. Her parents thought her being in a convent school away from home, she would learn to be more respectful of authority and less rebellious in her attitude. She hated the place. She could not adapt to the strict rules imposed on students like her. Besides, it was in a different country, a different culture with which she was trying to struggle even though her own culture was initially drawn from the Québécois ethnic culture. Micheline felt like une étrangère/a stranger in an environment that imposed more control, more rules and regulations by a group of nuns who used the iron rod to put their mark on their wards. Being an American, Micheline was branded an outsider by other students and une excitée by the nuns who had gotten it from the parents. She did her best not to act as what her mother had branded her, une excitée, a wild and an unruly one. The mother kept saying that her daughter, Micheline, was uncontrollable and unmanageable. Micheline tried to stick to the rules and regulations of the school but she often found herself in the middle of a conflict between being a "good girl" and a creative and rebellious spirit. It was really too much for her. She pleaded with her father to remove her from that institution, but her mother insisted that this was the best place for her daughter. A compromise was reached. Micheline would go to another school and this time it would be in northern Vermont, a school with proper credentials and no religious affiliation as well as no stringent rules. Micheline was allowed to be her own self, a young woman who explored her innate wanderings and provocative talents for being creative. Creativity had not been clearly defined for her. She knew that it existed and it was a definite part of her existence, but she could not define it as a goal in her young life. She knew that creativity meant delving in her imagination and her thoughts in order to scratch the surfaces and go beyond the surfaces and deep into her mind and her heart. The cerebral part would mean using her intellectual and inquisitive faculties while her heart meant the emotions and sensitive areas of her being. How does one reconcile both, she did not know yet, but wanted to explore the possibilities of both of them. That is why, later one, she would take courses in human development and choose a major called Human Development. She was especially interested in child development. She loved children. She told me that she intended not to embarrass nor hamper the growth of children with stringent rules and regulations. Her own mother was definitely not a model for her. She much preferred the creative musical side of her mother, a side that was rarely exposed and too often muted. She realized that her mother had been stunted all these years. By what and how? She could not explain. But it was there and Micheline had recognized it even when she was very young and often asking her mother to play the violin. She refused all the time. Was it the Catholic ethnic sacrifice linked with a very strong sense of duty? She did not know. Besides, she feared becoming like her mother, the dutiful, and religiously attached woman who committed herself to husband, family and home. That was the duty of every housewife and mother for Franco-American women. The children were the strong glue that held together le devoir, la religion et l'épouse/duty, religion, and wife. Spinsters were considered deprived of the basic qualities of a normal and married life. Those women belonged in a convent. It would be later on that Micheline would choose the University of Massachusetts then, afterwards, the University of Southern Maine to pursue her studies in Human Development and obtain her degree in it.

It was at the University of Massachusetts that she met several young men who were charmed by her beauty as a woman and her talents as a bright person. That's when she blossomed forth as an excitée, an incredibly active young woman with lots of friends and lots of energy. Her mother was not there to watch her every step of the way nor was she there intruding in her life and warning her not to be that excitée she so often accused her of being. Micheline once told me that when her mother told her "fais pas ton excitée", that meant stop living. Stop being yourself. It was during that time she met a young man she liked and had sex with him. The result was a pregnancy. It ended up being a girl. She refused to have an abortion and decided to give the baby away. She never pursued the outcome of this detachment. It was complete and unemotional. She had done the right thing, she told me. This way there were no complications, no obligations, and no restraints since she did not take the time and effort to be close to her child. It was years ago that I received an e-mail from a young woman who was looking for her birth mother and considered linking up with me to find out if Micheline Bousquet was that mother. Somehow through some records that she had located, she got the name Micheline Bousquet and matched that name with my name as a friend and correspondent. She wrote to me asking me about Micheline, her address and her personal information. She even sent me a digital photograph of herself. What I saw reminded me very much of Micheline as a young woman, I thought. I wasn't sure. I told Micheline about this encounter and she hardly accepted the fact that this young woman was her daughter. She told me that all of this was in the past and that she did not want to open up an unwanted wound. I let her be and never got in touch with the young woman. All I remember is that her lively and perky face resembled so much une excitée. I may have misjudged her. That was the end of that episode.

I never asked Micheline about her personal life including her sex life. All I know is that she met another young man, not of her ethnic group, and that the two got married and had two daughters, Monique and Mia. There did not seem to be much love in that marriage nor any father- ly relationship between father and daughters. Micheline eventually got a divorce and received no alimony and meager child support. I never knew the full name of that husband of hers except she called him John and she hardly spoke of him. All I know he visited her and her two girls in France with his wife. I could see that there was no closeness with the father whom they called l'Américain as the two girls looked at their mother somewhat furtively and smiled with a kind of a smirk. She struggled during those years and she did not in any way depend on her own family. She was an independent-minded woman. Her brother and her sister considered her as having abandoned the family. She corresponded for a while with her sister who traveled in Italy and delved into pottery. She did go and visit Miche- line in France once but there was no bonding of sisterly love, no closeness, no sharing of emotions. The sister returned home in Maine and has been living with her brother. Both parents died a few years apart. I had read the obituaries in the local papers. I'm the one who informed Micheline about these deaths. She did not come for the funerals but I did. All the mother, sister and brother wanted to know was Micheline's address. I did not give it to them. Micheline wanted to keep everything confidential.

Twice Micheline had brought her daughters to come and visit their grandparents here in Maine. She wanted them to get to know their grand- parents better and to create a bond between them. However, it never mate- rialized. It sounded to me that both Micheline's parents were not the affec- tionate kind nor did they initiate any bonding that could have lasted during the growing-up period of the young girls' lives and even gone beyond into their adulthood. Micheline was not surprised. She had expected something like that. Micheline and her daughters came to visit me during their stay in Maine while visiting the family, and I recognized a certain strain in the two girls's conversation about their grandparents. They indicated that both of them detected some quixotic behavior and odd bits of conversation. It was not what they had expected from their grandparents. The grandparents did not really know their grand kids for they had not communicated with them

for years if ever. It was somewhat an alienated relationship with no promise of ever becoming close and even intimate. The two girls had apparently
no well-cultivated relationships with neither father nor grandparents. They
did not know their paternal grandparents. The only closeness with another
person was Micheline their mother. Micheline had developed and nurtured
a very close relationship with her daughters and they appreciated this and
it grew to be intimate and loving.

In August 1987, I received a two-part long letter from Micheline
telling me about her experiences in Caux en basse Normandie and her
vernissage/preview, at La Galerie MICHEL on July 25. The exposition
was due to be opened from July 20 through August 2. It was situated in
Veules les Roses. Micheline related to me that one horticulturalist was fas-
cinated with one of her watercolors but that he did not have the adequate
funds to purchase it. She added in her letter that people were bouleversés/
bowled over, by her art work and her expression, her vision, and her ability
for giving to others the capacity of dreams[mon expression, ma vision,
et ma capacité à donner à autrui la capacité de rêver]. She also mentioned
that one has to be honest and strong facing a sponsor and that sponsors
are usually in promoting art for their own interest and glory. They usually
prefer a preview with champagne and canapés while she ordered simple
offerings like fruits and spring water.

Micheline admitted to me that she was not a city person but that
she needed city life, like Paris, for what it can offer. "I've not been very
equipped for building, only resisting. I'm tired of spending my energies
resisting." Then she adds, "I've realized that I must extricate myself from
Paris as soon as I have built there a connection, an opening that can be
nourished at a distance." Then she tells me that her goal is not to sell or
obtain recognition for her art is really not what fulfills her for fulfillment is
having a creative journey, giving inspiration and encouragement to others
for their own creative voyage. The letters from former students of hers
are what convinced her that the courses centered on creativity are what
inspired and delighted students. Then she tells me that she saw herself as a
"closet intellectual" and reading a variety of books as far as I can recall, she
says. "I now have interrogatory conclusions, workshops, demonstrating

concretely ma démarche/my procedure as to what concerns my ideas, and people react to this," she says.

Micheline then talks about colors in her watercolors. "Si la couleur est le support d'expression principale, il faut commencer la composition par des taches de couleurs et des taches naissent alors les lignes. Si l'on dessine d'abord les lignes, comme souvent nous avons appris, puis on y ajoute des couleurs, vous n'obtiendrez jamais un effet coloré ayant de l'unité et de la force. Les couleurs ont leurs propres dimensions et forces de rayonnement, et elles donnent aux surfaces d'autres valeurs que les lignes"/If color is the support of principal expression, one must start the composition with spots of color and from the spots are born the lines. If one draws the lines, first of all the lines, as we have often learned, then we add the colors, one will never obtain a colored effect having unity and strength. Colors have their own dimensions and strength of radiance and they give to surfaces other values than the lines. She then adds, "If only you could see, hear, interact with my students---it's as though I've offered another vision, another exposé." Finally, she ends her letter saying, "All my upbringing, my years of marriage sent me one message---I have nothing to offer. What if they have been all wrong, Norman? There has been a great deal of suffering, but look what I have been able to do with it."

The daughters, Monique and Mia, did not mind that their mother did not have a job after leaving the Oceanographic Museum in Monaco. Somehow Micheline found enough food and suitable housing for all three of them. Micheline admitted to me one day that there were times when she did not know if she could put sufficient food on the table or not. One night after an exhausting day of work and worries about getting her art supplies, she realized that all she had in the cupboard was a medium-size piece of bread. She would give it to the two girls with whatever they could find themselves and go without eating herself although she was starving for food. She went to bed hungry that night. Pas même un os à gruger.... not even a bone to gnaw on.

The three of them loved animals especially dogs. Later on, after Micheline had moved to Normandy, she got a large dog, a very large and adorable one. A shepherd dog, Micheline told me, a kind of animal that stomps around whom they named Boris. He was a large loving blubbering type animal that is easily loved and cared for. He had long grey hair hanging over his eyes. I would have cut it off so that the poor animal would be able to see more clearly. However, I was told that would not be healthy for this kind of dog. Good, I thought, let him look like a huge hairy, floppy and slow-stomping dog. Micheline liked him that way. He became her close friend and support for her lack of friends that love you and take care of not offending you while mending the pains and ills of being lonely due to a lack of male intimacy in her life. However, her constant problem before she made Normandy her home was moving and making sure her daughters had a steady schedule that included schooling.

After Nice, Micheline moved with her daughters to a suburb near Paris. She took what she could afford. It was a huge quadrangle of mortar and bricks built speedily without comfort and outdoor natural beauty. She hated it and thought that the environment was conducive to living in jail without bars but with the constraints of fear and sometimes panic. The three of them did not feel free there nor did they want to be closed in like animals in a zoo. The neighborhood was not the least friendly. When the girls were at school, Micheline wandered around to find better housing and favorable environment. She was determined to seek a more delightful area where the girls would play at ease and do their assignments with peace and tranquility of mind. As for her, she would relish a quiet, inspiring and welcoming environment where she would be able to exercise her creativity and work on her watercolors. It would indeed be a quest but she was up to it. She was determined to find a place that would meet her expectations and needs of being an artist.

Micheline sought locations and available housing and read many a catalog and brochure that would invite her to explore the proposed or recognized town, village or small rural area. She would have preferred a place near the seashore like the northern part of Normandy where Monet had painted away from Paris and other large cities. She wondered if she would ever find such a place. She did. It was situated in the northwestern part of Normandy near the English Channel facing the Cliffs of Dover where Claude Monet had found his plein air painting spot. The commune was called Varengeville-sur-mer. Monet had found this spot near the cliffs and produced Impressionist paintings, one called La maison du douanier de Varengeville[the custom house]. The village has a small 13th Century church called Saint-Valéry with a small adjoining cemetery where Georges Braque is buried.

Micheline decided to explore the commune and discover its history of painters, adventurers and writers. She liked the environment as described in the small catalog for tourists. It was exactly what she was looking for. Would she be able to afford it, she asked herself. Would she find the needed housing for the three of them. Would the girls like moving there. They had moved so many times that she was sure they would adapt to it. Furthermore, this move would certainly be a better one than the move to la commune de béton, the cement one. She would consult with them as usual since she did not like making decisions on her own. She wanted to give her daughters choices and a chance to express their likes and dislikes. They knew that she always did the best for them. They were not the rebelling kind. She knew they were not des excitées. So, one Friday afternoon in May after class had ended, dismissing the Saturday morning classes, Micheline and her two daughters took the train for Dieppe whose train station served Varengeville-sur-mer. The air was pure, the soft breeze welcomed them and the radiance of the day shone like a bright star in the heavens. They knew they were home. From Dieppe they took a taxi to the village of Varengeville. Micheline took her daughters to la mairie, the official town hall, to inquire about living there. The lady in charge told Micheline that there were very few residences for sale and none for rent. Most of the residents had lived in Varengeville for years and many were from the larger cities and spent their summers in Varengeville. She suggested they go elsewhere. Micheline told her that she had in mind Varengeville since it was ideal for artists like herself. Knowing she was an artist, the clerk opened up to Micheline and suggested she return to the village a bit later when she would have done some searches for housing for her. Micheline thanked her and withdrew to a beautiful garden known as Les Bois de Moutiers where visitors were invited for a fee to wander around this splendid garden of flowers and plants. Micheline told the woman collecting the fees that she did not have the money to enter the garden. The woman took a long look at the two girls and felt sympathetic toward them and the mother. They looked like a charming threesome, she told them. Since the park had few visitors that day, she told them that she would allow them in for free. She could not bear to send them away without visiting such a lovely spot in Varengeville. Besides, she felt a certain obligation to artists, she told Micheline when Micheline revealed to her that she did watercolors. Varengeville was known to attract artists, she told Micheline. The three of them, mother and daughters, ate their sandwiches and fruits and talked about the possibility of moving to Varengeville.

The following week, the three of them returned to Varengeville only to find out that there was absolutely nothing available for them. The girls were terribly disappointed while Micheline told them that she was not giving up. She was determined to settle in Varengeville-sur-mer and no place else. I knew Micheline as a willful, determined and absolutely intent on finding a solution to anything to which she set her mind. This time her artist livelihood depended on it. Varengeville, here we come, she said out loud not even turning around to look at the beautiful garden they had visited in early afternoon. It was a delightful garden with its charming flowers some of which came from far away places such as the rhodo-dendrums almost reaching full bloom, the stately calla lilies, the rich and joyous magnolias, the sparkling clematis, and the exotic Japanese irises as well as the budding roses. There were some for every season, she was told. The delightful and stately Japanese maple appeared with its bright colors in November. That was something to look forward to, she thought. Although Micheline was not a flower person as an artist, she recognized the value of the rich splendor of the colors of every flower. Colors were the bright spark of life for Micheline and flowers represented an entire panoply of various colors and different hues that she associated with butterflies and the haunting range of birds in their splendor of colors. Micheline recognized the fact that parks such as that of the Moutiers were a fine example of nature's glory in bloom. A fine and delightful display of radiant colors that was truly an iconic moment of inspiration for her. Micheline could not resist colors. They were the trigger of her creativity. Watercolor was her medium while colors were her spark of creative soul energy. Micheline told me once that she got her artistic energy from her soul through colors. That's why she let the colors flow on their own in a watercolor. They found their way on the Arche paper and guided her in the eventual making of the work of art. That was Micheline's theory of watercolor art.

And so, it was decided that Micheline would return to Varengeville in order to pursue the search for housing even though the lady at the mairie as well as several women she had talked to about a place to stay had all insisted that there were no houses for sale and no place to rent. Everything was taken by summer visitors and tourists. Except an old deserted boulangerie that lay dormant on a small corner of a laid-over field. Micheline was determined to find a place no matter what, be it a deserted boulangerie, an abandoned mill or even a dilapidated barn. Something, quelque chose, simplement quelque chose d'habitation, she whispered to her daughters. Well, she found that something. It was indeed an abandoned bakery once owned by a popular baker in the village until he died and left the property to a niece who lived in a small village around Carcassonne. The relative wanted no part of the estate, refused to pay the back taxes and so the property was turned over to the village lawyer who had very little interest in selling the property. Why he did not even want to discuss it with Micheline who insisted that she wanted the property for herself and her two daughters even though she knew she had very few assets if none.

Micheline was so determined to buy the old bakery that she plunged into a feverish project of paperwork and time-demanding work of research in property and banking regulations. It was a grueling project but she put all of her energies into it. She spent hours upon hours delving into records, files, and regulations until she came up with a written proposal that she presented to the town lawyer. At first, he refused to read the long script. Micheline kept insisting until the lawyer, wanting to get rid of her in his office, decided to give her an interview. He realized that she had put much time and effort into her proposal and that it was worth a reading and a face-to-face talk with the woman who kept insisting that her proposal was legal, reasonable and financially sound. The lawyer realized that he was dealing with an intelligent and reasonable person. She showed the lawyer how resourceful she could be given the circumstances and challenges facing her. For her, it was a question of do or die, as they say. It truly was a question of getting the property or ending her search for a place where she could do her artwork in peace and tranquility without any thoughts of moving again and becoming a nomad as well as a living twisted soul. The girls had told her that they were getting tired of ever-changing living place and that they had had it with temporary dwellings and forever packing up to move. She understood that and she herself had the same thoughts. It was time to settle down and enjoy some sense of permanence and contentment in life. She also understood that the artist is often on the move. However, she had had enough of wanderings and living precariously. "Enough is enough," she told me. "Moving creatively is real", she said, "but moving because you are not well situated is for the birds. Birds move all the time."

She then took her challenge with her two hands and worked tirelessly day and night to come up with a proposal that would be legal, fair and honest. First of all, she had to find a bank and banker to accept her proposal. The town lawyer had insisted on that since she would need an agreement on a mortgage. I received an aérogramme from her dated March 1, 1989 telling me she had just bought a house. It's definitely worthwhile quoting her letter here with a proper translation of certain parts for those who do not read French. Here it is: "J'ai une sacré nouvelle à t'annoncer…es-tu bien assis?/I have some awfully good news to tell you… are you sitting down? "I have just bought a small house here on this same road but next to the Parc des Moutiers. I've been working on this in Sept. but did not want to mention any of it during these months because I've had to negotiate as I never have for anything…get through lies that the vendeurs claimed in order to keep the price high, 400.000 fr. though these months I was a 'helluva' detective with the help of others, bien sur/of course, and then once getting the price down to 280,000 fr. I then had to find a bank to give me a mortgage & take a risk on me----I went through 8 bankers----getting no's and more no's, finally I wrote up the equivalent of a grant proposal with a marketing study & plan based on comparative market analyses of what I've accomplished since Jan.'87. One small bank was finally so impressed & respectful of my efforts to be "sérieuse" that they said, yes! I should sign the final bill of sales "acte de vente" by the 15th or 25th of this month---I plan to diversify my work into regional expression & also keep my atelier ouvert ou publique/keep my workshop open or public. "Il y a 40,000 visiteurs au Park des Moutiers & another 15,000 easy who walk by my little house every year. No one else has what I'm offering & this is based on Varengeville being a cultural tourist attraction---no one even sells nice postcards!!"

"Since seeing this little house I've felt it was the next important step even though everyone told me it would be impossible ---I had no money, no salary, etc. etc. etc. Norman, I don't know what happened to me but I just couldn't accept it would be impossible---I've had to put out a lot of creative energy, creative problem solving---but the whole step is accomplished---buying the little house(I will send you photos soon)---now I have to follow through my ideas---my mortgage payments are only 400fr more than I pay for rent---over a 15yr period---I am thrilled & over-whelmed & would like to say merde à tous ceux qui pensent que je suis incompétente, rêveuse sans aboutir,"/shit to all those who think that I am incompetent, full of dreams, without any results... etc.etc.
"Other good things are going on with workshops, galeries--"

What Micheline proposed was a way of purchasing the land and the delapidated building and financing the deal with income that she proposed getting through the sales of her works of art. She had in hand written proposals of sales from either art dealers or individual buyers who were interested in her art. Micheline had managed to obtain enough signa-tured agreements to ensure sufficient income for the sale along with the indentured promises of future payments. Besides, she showed the bankers that she had successfully accomplished her task of marketing and selling her art work. She had demonstrated her skills not only as an artist but as an accountant and an expert in comparative marketing analyses.

She was so sure of herself that her self-confidence ran higher than it had ever been. She had earned it after all. Good women like her attack a problem like someone wages war. They go at it with determination if not passion. Every step is measured by assurance and rational concentration. There are no deviations, no false pride in determining the results. Every calculation is measured and brought to bear in a determined and willful way. Strong-willed people do not deviate from their goal and they do not give in to apparent impossible challenges. Micheline was a woman of determination and willpower. She did not abandon what appeared to her as an impossible task. Impossible was not in her vocabulary. She had a knack of turning the impossible on its heels and making it possible. That's the way it was with her. That was her amazing talent.

Of course, Micheline did not always succeed in her attempts to gain control over every single challenge that came her way. Just like the time a local grocer had warned her about her tab and she had delayed paying him until he simply cut off the supplies she wanted. He did it in spite of her pleading and promises to settle her account. The cupboard was bare for quite some time. Then came the sales of three watercolors and she was determined that paying the grocer was a high priority.

Micheline worked tirelessly at her art as well as her duty as a mother and provider knowing full well that duty, devoir, the Franco-American anthem call was persistently on her mind and in her heart. Of course, she tried desperately to rid herself of imposed values such as devoir but nevertheless this one was ever anchored in her sort de femme, her womanly fate. She knew that and struggled to at the very least partly rid herself of it. After all, she could not rid herself of the very core of her existence as "la petite Canadienne" as the French called her. Cultural values are like unmistakable adhesives that even time refuses to render null and void. They are the glue that holds everything together as an integral part of the heritage.

Chapter THREE :

OF OILS AND DOLDRUMS

IN HER LETTER dated May 21, 1990 from Grenoble, Micheline mentions that she suffered from doldrums at times. They were caused by a strange feeling of vagueness and out of sorts. Here is what she says, "C'est évident que je passe depuis quelque temps un creux dans la vague/it's evident that for some time now I've been going through a kind of ebbtide---I've just not had the energy to pick myself up or if sad when I seem to have some----il y a quelque chose qui se présente pour m'enfoncer/there is something that presents itself to bring me down. Maybe it's a bad year for Libras."

Then she goes on to tell me that in January she decided to expand her creative expression and begin"after all this time" to paint in oils. She admits that she has to be careful with oils since the solvents are lethal for her and that she tries to paint outside as much as she can or with all the doors and windows open. She goes on to say that she is discovering or rediscovering oils while she has not abandoned watercolors at all.

Micheline relates that her teaching in Grenoble is coming to an end this particular year with an exhibit of her Grenoble students'works. She is hoping that it will draw more students for the following year. She goes on to tell me that she has not sold any of her works since last summer and that the workshop is open again but very few people are coming in spite of the publicity. "I don't know what to think. I'm so tired of living in the moments of financial crises," she adds, "never having enough or always anxious because I'm overdrawn in order to survive---& yet I am unable to go out & sell myself---present my works, etc. etc. etc. I don't know why I am so blocked---the person who had seemed so interested here in Grenoble has given no further sign of life---I don't know what to think---he had given me a rendezvous but never showed, never called to explain & I haven't been courageous enough to contact him either. In June when I finish my last course here---I plan & will see him if he'll see me---but just his doing that---shattered me---I guess I'm not able with my art to accept rejection---as much as I've been able to fight in the past about other things, I've never been able to go out & easily show my work & absolutely unable to hunt out an art agent which is what I need desperately before I drown... and I cannot pass into action. My semi-paralysis of my arm and head seem to have stabilized---I have moments of great fatigue---épuisement/worn out." I wasn't aware of her situation and her mental state. She certainly had her problems, the greatest one being poor all based on her lack of sales of her works. She knew she had to put in more effort into the marketing end but it wasn't in her to pursue such an avenue. As she says, she had the talent and the drive to make things happen but did not have it for publicity and especially sales of her product. She simply expected that people would recognize her talent as an artist and buy her paintings since she recognized them as truly worthwhile if not outstanding. After all, she was the one, the artist and teacher, who had blazed the way in revealing her amazing talent as a watercolorist and artist of consequence. Why, one could say that she was in the league of a Turner and Kadinski. I would.

Micheline then tells me that she's returning to Varengeville and is happy to return home. Then she adds, "I'm trying to resurrect myself but un passage vide/ an empty passage is horrible...I know I need to rise to the occasion & what is it that keeps me so down in the doldrums. Sometimes I feel I'm not like me anymore...Corinne my next door neighbour---Robert Mallet's wife (Parc des Moutiers) tried to commit suicide 3-4 weeks ago and that for some reason or rather m'a bouleversée et continue à me travailler, je ne sais pourquoi"/it shattered me and continues to work itself in me. I don't know why.

She then told me that her sister was getting a divorce and was coming to Varengeville for a couple of months that summer. Micheline told me that her sister was struggling with a lot of issues. I did not know anything about that. I had never met her sister except to find out from Micheline that her sister had spent some time in Italy trying to mend a marriage that was failing and perhaps broken. I didn't even know her name. The reason she was spending time in Italy was that she was trying to learn pottery and was quite good at it. However, what I learned about the Bousquet family was that neither father, mother, sister nor brother including Micheline, none of them experienced a happy relationship either with one another or with someone else. And that started when they were young all the way through their upbringing. Was it a dysfunctional family? I do not really know except at times Micheline gave me some inkling of disunity or disharmony as well as a lack of sincere affection on the part of any of them. I thought it was a truly sad case of family turbulence, I would say. It seems to me that not one of them could stand one another. Micheline told me later on that she was glad when her sister left. Evidently there was no affection there even though she was her only sister and she had not seen her in a long while. I do not know how the sister was received by the two daughters but they did not want to be with their aunt nor did they appreciate her marriage difficulties. That's all she talked about according to Micheline. Did the two sisters talk at all about their art and craft. It seems to me that this would have been a excellent time to share their fruitful artistic endeavors. No, the sister becried her Italian husband while Micheline tried to console her. That was the extent of the sisterly encounter. At least, that's what Micheline told me. There was also a brother who stayed at home with the parents, but that's yet another matter. I do not like family brouille/misunderstandings.

Micheline also mentions the "care" package that she received from me and that the two daughters raved about. This was not the first time I had done that. It was an expensive thing what with the postage exceptionally high. I did it to please the girls and especially to raise Micheline's morale. The three of them rarely enjoyed treats like Fluff Marshmallow, peanut butter, MaryAnn candies, Skybars and soft footies as well as warm gloves that I included in their "care" packages. Whatever I thought about that would delight them especially for Christmas. Everyone loves surprises. It makes the heart glad.

Now as for doldrums, the word refers to the ocean regions near the equator characterized by calms or light winds. The definition I found that refers to what Micheline uses means a period or spell of listlessness or depression. It appears to me that Micheline realizes that she was now and then confronted with depression. Was that a recurring thing? I do not know but I do know that living the life she was leading was enough to depress anyone what with no family encouragement, hard work mixed with the realization that it was seldom rewarded by acceptance by others in terms of sales which was her livelihood, dreams of someday being accepted by other artists into their ranks especially by the Parisian clique or crowd, the intolerable sense of being poor, mortgage payments and bills that were ever waiting for her, and the never ending torture of having to satisfy her needs as an artist, psychologically, esthetically and financially were all phases of her growing depression, I think. Micheline knew deep down that she was indeed an artist of great consuming talent but people did not seem to fully realize her strength and determination to become worthy of some fame and fortune. Not that she was a greedy person but she craved for artistic recognition and the rewards of an earnest and sincere desire to fulfill not only her dream as a talented artist but her passion to teach people how to be creative and succeed in their endeavors be they art, crafts, words, pottery, or even dog training. Anything! Micheline had within her soul the express desire and want to participate fully in the game called life and life to her meant creativity. When all of this was depreciated by whatever, fate, rules and regulations, or even people who did not understand creativity, then depression set in. It meant that the soul was going through a kind of listlessness or a demoralizing spurt of broken dreams that rendered the human being whoever she/he was cut off from what Wordsworth once said poetically "the splendor in the grass." Once that splendor is gone then depression sets in. It's a terrible thing to become listless and without luster. And that's what it meant to Micheline when her mother used to warn her about being a lively one, "fais pas ton excitée," she used to tell her. Tout cela gruge et bouscule l'âme et la rend morbide et déprimée," I would say---All of that gnaws and shatters the soul and renders it morbid and depressed. Gawd, I'm beginning to sound like Baudelaire.

In her letter dated March 12, 1991 from Varengeville, Micheline thanks me for the "care" package that took a very long time getting there due to possibly a postal strike(they often have them in France) and announces that she has not been feeling well psychologically speaking. She says, "I've written to you often during these past months---the letters go unfinished or unmailed---they are so 'down & out'---they depress me even more than when I wrote them." Then she tells me that she is facing a crucial problem. She admits that she is going through an existential crisis that only she can get out of it. But, she adds, "I'm not the only one who can relate to this type of suffering & I am begining to feel less isolated, less alone--- though instinctly feeling we are in a way alone on this trip called 'life'." Then she goes on to say, "Meaningfulness is a long, long word---& I don't know what it means!" Then she goes from English to French, a cultural part of being Franco-American like me. "L'acceptation de ça est difficile-- -l'acceptation de soi-même---je n'accepte pas mais je commence un peu au moins de considérer---je n'accepte pas que je peux être dans un gouffre--- incapable de saisir comment sortir et encore moins capable d'accepter des conseils des autres qui ne sont pas eux-mêmes là---pas que je souhaiterais ceci à quiquonque---mais c'est toujours plus facile de dire à une autre de se secouer. La dépression n'est pas si secouable que ça---et en plus je pense que la seule façon de m'en sortir et de l'accepter---." This must have been a very difficult letter to write. Anyway, here is the translation of the upper part of her letter: Acceptance of this is difficult---the acceptance of oneself---I do not accept but I'm beginning a bit to at least consider it---I do not accept that I could be in a chasm---incapable of grasping how to get out of it and much less capable of of accepting the counsels of others who are not even there themselves---not that I would wish that to whomever---but it's always easier to say to another one to shake it off. Depression is not so easy to shake off as that---and moreover I think that the only way of getting out of it and accept---.

Then Micheline informs me that her workshops are going well and with success. Her students recognize her immense talent and wish to bring it up in class. She tells me that she has 19 students in Annecy, 13 in Grenoble and 6 in Paris. However, she also tells me that she is still struggling with her finances. She keeps falling behind. She doesn't sell enough paintings in order to meet her obligations of borrowing and spending. She tells me that she is less and less able to do commercial work. So, she spends most of her time in the workshops with delightful students and gathers the love and affection of people around her which she needs in order to live with caring and love. But, that does not solve the problem of finances.

What enlightens me about her psychological situation is when she writes, "Je panique chaque fois lorsque je fais un bond en avant et c'est insupportable la peur et panique existant dans moi quand il y a des signes d'affection ou amour vers moi d'autrui---j'ai pris conscience récemment---je fais les choses autant entier que je peux---(ex. mes cours, mes élèves) quand je commence à saisir que je suis aimée soit par mes élèves, toi, d'autres---je sens un danger insupportable et je commence à m'éloigner par toutes sortes de manoeuvres---j'ai pris conscience dernièrement car une élève que je respecte beaucoup m'a parlé de la qualité de mon travail avec les élèves---et que je suis très fortement aimée---au lieu de vivre ça avec joie---j'ai été saisie moralement et physiquement d'une panique qui est encore là." Translation: I panic each time when I take a leap forward and it's insupportable the fear and panic that exist in me when there are signs of affection or love towards me from others---I recently became aware--I do things in their entirety as much as I can---(ex. my courses, my students) when I begin to grasp that I am loved by my students, you, others---I feel an insupportable danger and I begin to m'éloigner/get away by all kinds of maneuvers-- I became aware recently of a student that I respect a lot who talked to me about the quality of my work with students---and that I am strongly loved---instead of living that with joy---I was seized morally and physically with a panic that is still there.

Micheline talked about this with her sister who is actually in therapy and is aging with a surprising quickness. She tried to make Micheline understand that she experienced a blockage due to her lack of relationship with her mother. That her growing up years were filled with affective dangers. That at this time and place Micheline was reliving her adolescence with her two daughters who were in the middle of their own adolescent years. That it is not difficult to love your children whatever the difficulties and the ambivalences in the life of a mother. That her daughters are the only ones in whom she has an affective confidence because they come out of her. There is a kind of symbiosis that allows her to psychologically feel the confidence she needs even if everything seems paradoxal, she tells me. She knows that she must reach the bottom of her problem because she feels there is a route that will bring her out of her problem but she has not found it yet. She admits that she feels frozen almost paralyzed because she realizes that's the root of her depression. How to get rid of the cause of one's depression is the enigma that she has to solve one way or another. But how? When I put the letter down I felt sorry for Micheline and sad, sad that I could not help her, be there when she needed someone with whom she could share in person her terrible pain of being psychologically bouleversée/ torn and shattered.

In her letter dated January 9, 1992, Micheline wished me a Happy New Year! and talked about her artistic activities. It's a long letter of seven large pages. At times she skips writing to me but as the weeks go by she then realizes that she has not written in a long time and then decides to send me a letter that she had planned on sending weeks before. I never felt rejected or forgotten by her. I knew she was busy and had many cares and concerns especially about finances. I tried to help her as much as I could and once in a while sent her some euros that I had or gotten through the bank. She never begged, never told me I should send her money. I knew of her low income and her financial obligations. I knew she worried a lot. I did what I could but I could have done more. I always wondered why her parents, her brother did not help out. There was a breach in their relationship and it was never mended. There was no compassion nor any sense of family members helping family members. It seemeed very sad to me since one of the values of Franco-Americans is la famille and the family is of major importance. One key note could be said like this, on s'entr'aide dans la famille car la famille c'est le coeur d'une société qui honore et valorise la famille. Pas faire cela serait comme arracher le coeur ou le briser en morceaux. ---we help one another in the family since the family is the heart of a society that honors and sets value on the family. Not to do this would be like pulling out the heart or breaking it in pieces./ On lui avait arraché le coeur à Micheline dès son enfance, je crois. I believe that Micheline's heart was pulled out right at her childhood days.

At the end of her letter she did write as an addendum, "I forgot! The day before Noël j'ai reçu enfin ma 'Carte de Résidence' au lieu d'une Carte de séjour---ça veut dire que j'ai presque toutes les mêmes droits qu'une française et Monique et Mia pourront faire des études et travailler!!! It was fantastic!!! Tu t'imagines???" translation: I received at last my residency card instead of the reidence permit---it means that I have almost all of same rights that a French woman has, and Monique and Mia will be able to do their studies and work!.....Can you imagine that?

The gist of the letter deals with her workshops and travels in France. For example there is Annecy, the Venice of the Alps. A splendid city of castles, cathedrals and canals near Lake Annecy. It's a real tourist attraction and draws thousands of visitors annually. It's the largest city of the Haute-

Savoie department in the Auvergne-Rhône-Alpes region of Southeastern France. It's known as the Pearl of French Alps. Annecy attracted Micheline's attention as a good location to draw students to her workshops. Art and creativity were two drawing cards and Micheline had the aces. She met people that introduced her to possible devotees to art and she set up an exhibition there in 1991 with Anne Lemaire who did pastels. Micheline offered her huiles---oils. The vernissage/ preview occured Friday December at 18 h 30. Inside the brochure for the exhibition is one of Micheline's finest oil paintings. It's unnamed but I would call it "The red plume." It's a large bright ever eye-catching bright red plume-like insert in the middle of blue swerling cloud-like growths. The red plume emerges or extends as a pink burst on the very top of the red plume going right up to the edge. It's a fascinating work of art. It reminds me of Eugène Delacroix, one of the leading artists of the French Romantic period of the 19th century. He had a passion for the exotic and for color. He emphasized color and movement rather than clarity of outline and form. This is one of his quotes that deals with color: "Not only can color which is under fixed laws, be taught like music, but it is easier to learn than drawing whose elaborate principles cannot be taught." This, in a way, reminds me of Micheline Bousquet and her philosophy of painting, color before drawing lines.

Coming back to the color red in Micheline's painting, I am reminded of Delacroix's use of red such as in "Liberty Guiding the People" with the bright red in the three-part French flag. In his painting "The Lion Hunt" we see the bright red cloak of one of the hunters and in "The Barque of Dante" there's the bright red headgear of Dante that strikes you. Although Micheline was not a follower of the classical artists, I see some influence here of a Delacroix and color. I love this particular painting of hers for its somber variegated background and especially what I call the vivid red plume. Chacun à son goût.

As for the workshops Micheline tells me that she guided/facilitated a ten-day creativity workshop for ten students. She says that she did not teach any painting techniques but that she talked about the spirit of the artist and the truth of the research rather than the research of a truth. She says, " I found this approach much more gratifying & whole & have begun incorporating this approach in my regular courses. Because creating isn't easy & assez complexe ---there is an automatic selection occuring in my students---for me this is excellent even si ça réduit mes effectives---if it reduces my numbers----at least I'm surrounded by people who are engaged with themselves & not just with outward appearances. I had also come to a point in my workshops & extended course to the point where I hated going, hated teaching & yes even hated most of my students. I was severely criticized a few months ago by someone whom I respect beaucoup for turning out technicians, people who believed themselves artists and living my courses as well as my painting with a desire to please."Pour faire l'histoire courte, je veux simplement que tu saches que j'ai eu très mal et avec honnêteté savais que ma douleur était parce que cette personne avait touché en moi une vérité"/in order to make the story short, I simply want you to know that I felt very bad and honestly I knew what my pain was because this person had touched in me a truth.

Micheline goes on to say that this was how her oils got a 'helluva' lot better as well as her courses. Then she says that she is no longer painting nor teaching to please, to try to sell especially to have people say what a good artist the teacher is. Then she adds, "Ce n'est pas une question d'être bonne ou performante en quelque chose, mais d'être totalement présente et authentique même si les gens te rejettent"/It's not a question of being good or performing in something, but being totally present and authentic even if people reject you.

She then admits that she had gone through a lot and that much of her depression was "right on." She was not being herself, she adds, without placing value judgments, usually negative. "This step," she adds, "has been so arduous, so painful---why is it so---because once we make the step it's difficult to understand how we could have been in the previous world---it's all related to my childhood & always hearing 'arrête de faire ton excitée!' ----well, je suis une excitée , une passionnée, intense, impossible, avec des opinions et très cabochard/but that's me & I have to accept me & have to live me in all that I do---my painting is so me, I don't even understand me or it & feel there is something mysterious but incomprehensible. I'm just no longer able to keep 'mon excitation' in check. You understand a bit?"/stop being the wild one, well I am wild, a passionate one, intense, impossible and with my own opinions and very hardheaded.

Then Micheline tells me that she has closed her workshop to the public and only receives people by appointment and those that she wants. She then says that an artist also needs a refuge and must know that protecting oneself is also necesary for there is no shame in wanting that. She then adds, "Ce n'est pas facile de s'assumer jusqu'au bout d'une passion ni d'une passionnée...mais l'autre choix est de mourir dans son intérieur---ce que j'avais pas probablement réalisé jusqu'ici c'est de ne pas s'accepter (even when it is most uncomfortable for others) nous pouvons faire rien jusqu'au bout. J'ai encore peur, peut-être plus que jamais car je sais maintenant que je ne peux pas reculer...ni dans ma vie surtout pas dans ma peinture qui est ma vie!"/It's not easy to come to terms with up to the end of a passion nor a passionate one...but the other choice is to die in one's interior---what I did not probably realize up until now was not to accept oneself we can do nothing up to the end. I'm still afraid, possibly more than ever for I know now that I cannot back up...neither in my life especially in my painting which is my life.

Micheline then informs me that she has fifteen oils on exhibit in Annecy---all painted with all the wholeness she could muster up to that point. She needed to see them in an exhibition space she liked and have the recul[stepping back] to see them and see their history. After she finished hanging them, she went for a walk and returned alone and looked and looked and let herself feel. She was pleased knowing that one must always continue. It was strong, she said, and representative of herself. She had not cheated, she added.

The people's reaction was varied, from diabolical to mysterious incredible force. People were uncomfortable yet stayed in front of works unable to move on to the next out of fear perhaps of what the self would be, she told me. "Paintings are something transparent when the artist does not cheat with herself. People don't have to like it," she declares. "But if one stirs an emotion whatever it may be," she says, "tant mieux et si pas tant pis, peut-être un autre jour."/so much the better and if not, too bad, probably another day.

Micheline then talks about following similar ideas of the Renaissance in terms of multiple superpositions of colors to give depth to the oil. She says that she has taken from their basic technique, improvised in her way, using contrasts of light and the work seems to give off light even in a darkened room. She adds that given the available pigments today, her colors are much more varied than in the Renaissance and the subtleties interesting.

She then asked me for a couple of books and told me about her two children beginning to mature and have their own wings to fly by themselves. "Both have their passion," she says, "and I think I've been able to give them that which I had a hard time giving to myself because it certainly wasn't in our childhood that our dreams & passion were nourished."

Micheline tells me that she was touched by my two passages that I sent her regarding her work. "Il y a même, si j'ai des grands moments de silence, une complicité de passion---I know you understand & even though I may have great insecurity, je sais que tu es toujours là pour échanger ce que tu es avec moi"/I know that you are always there to exchange what you are to me---not to be abandoned in your darkest moments is something very precious & I ask myself why for even I have great moments of silence, a complicity of passion.

Afterwards, she tells me about the triptich she made which, she claims, has a lot of force and mystery. "Je me demande, what I do---I don't know, I just do! Un tableau a rien à signifier, il est. Et c'est cette gratuité qui lui donne une force dans le temps."/A painting has nothing to signify, it is. And this gratuity that gives it a force in time. She ends the letter hoping that I will finally be published. It will happen because it's "vrai". "Il faut du courage, de la passion et du culot!!" she adds./You need courage, passion and nerve/cheek.

The reader might wonder how many letters did she write. A lot spaced over a long period of time. Sometimes I would write to her, send her "care" packages and other things. I would wait and wait for some signal of life. I never gave up on her. I trusted that she would eventually get in touch with me and write me a long letter telling me the latest news and new works of art. We became very close friends as you can see by her letters and she was ever frank about it. I was the springboard for her trials in art and human sharing. There was never any personal passion between us just the passion of creativity, the best kind. Friendship is best established when authenticity and trust are at the root of it. I do not know where she is right now or even if she is still alive. I simply wish her good fortune and good dreams. This biography is my testimony of her influence on me and so many creative souls as well as her love for someone who as a stranger at first became a close and true friend. I miss her terribly.

September 9, 1992---Micheline writes about her workshops in Annecy, Grenoble and later in Paris with some Americans. She then adds that she spent the entire month of August holding a creativity workshop. "Many times I ask myself if it's very honest what I teach or do? The more I do this the more I really wonder---si la graine de potentiel créatrice n'est pas là, on peut-il la semer?"/if the seed of potential creative is not there can one sow it? she asks. She teaches two levels, one and two. The beginning level deals with perceptual, emotional, intellectual & cultural barriers that forms creativity as well as the difference between creativity and creation.

Being creative does not insure a creation, she adds.

Micheline also talks about a student of hers who told her that she had gone to a retreat somewhere in Isère. The student told her that she had thought about her over and over again and if she continued to hold back her energies in her paintings, in her work with students, she would auto-destruct. "Il faut que j'arrête d'avoir peur," she says.---I must stop being afraid. She adds, "Whenever I've been my passionate self I've been rejected at some level---rejecion is a narcissistic blessure--wound---can I ever get beyond mon nombril??---my belly button, she asks. She then says that she was disappointed in not being able to travel this summer. This must have been a veritable deception for her.

I had told Micheline that I wanted to do her genealogy and she sent me this information: BOUSQUET, Jean-Joseph, né 21 mars 1911 à Trois-Rivières ou Joliet de : Amédée Bousquet, Henriette Pratt.   SAMSON: Marie Rita, née 15 septembre 1910 à Manchester, N.H. de Émile Samson et Henriette Cormier. That's all she could remember. This means that her father was Canadian and her mother American. I never succeeded in doing her full genealogy.

I received the following letter dated January 10, 1994 telling me that she had gone to Nice to celebrate Ben's 50th birthday and surprised both Ben and Janine by her unexpected presence there. They had been friends for a number of years ever since they worked at the Oceanographic Museum in Monaco. Micheline made the trip with joy and was very happy to meet both husband and wife that she had not seen for a long time. She forgot her depression or I should say she put it aside and revived her fond memories of two friends who had supported her in so many ways. I would say, De vrais amis ça adoucit le coeur et la souffrance/true friends soften the heart and suffering. That was the case for Micheline, the troubled and bewildered creative artist. She did have friends but not the ones she could confide in about her lack of open trust with someone she was able to discuss her stages of depression. She was indeed an excitée and no one understood that except people like me who could link the word with Franco-American cultural values. There are words that convey specific meanings or particular ideas and one has to have lived these values and meanings to fully understand the full significance or suggestive nuances of these words. The mother did to a certain extent by warning her not to be a wild one and Micheline kept telling people that she was an excitée because that was in her nature and she lived it. I would say that being an excitée was part of her being and living as she often said. For her being "wild" was an integral part of being creative. She never denied that. Apparently her mother never understood that. Her mother linked that to crossing the line of good behavior and obedience to parents and elders. Her parents supported the values of calm, straightforward and dutiful behavior that reflect a good upbringing. All of this was measured in terms of following the ever-lasting demands of one's heritage. Besides, it reflected on the parents and their pride in raising their children dutifully. Micheline was seen as a rebel and une excitée. That was indeed a black mark against her. At least that's what Marie Rita, the mother, thought. The refusal to play her violin was perhaps her punishment and her justification in bringing up strong, proper and obedient children. After all, the family reputation was at stake. One never knows about the thoughts and behavior of mothers, especially Franco-American mothers.

Going down south also meant Micheline could revive memories about the areas where she and her daughters had lived and where they had experienced their débarquement in France : Vence, Villefranche and Saint-Jean-Cap-Ferrat. Vence was the location where they first landed. She admits that seeing these places brought tears to her eyes. "Mon dieu! Je ne sais pas comment j'ai vraiment 'construit' ma vie même avec toutes les faillles depuis ce temps...I've come a long long way & have to start realizing that et à fond"/My God! I don't know how I really constructed my life even with all of the flaws of that time.

Micheline goes on to say, "I've not done it alone, Dieu a mis des gens sur mon chemin pour assurer mon passage---mais je n'ai pas refuser le chemin"/God has put some people on my road to insure the passage, but I have not refused the road. "Why have I been so destructive of myself in not accepting my construction. Il y a toujours plus à faire, mais il faut aussi savoir regarder lucidement à ce qui a été construit"/There is always more to do, but one must also know how to look lucidly at what has been constructed.

"I also realized that I have a damn good class of contacts of certain persons. You are and have been someone on the sidelines, but so important---in looking analytically, you entered, stage left as Mme Roche went out, stage right---et tu as eu la même conviction dans moi, qu'elle---que j'étais une artiste & a good one & had something to say and you had the same conviction in me as she did---that I was an artist and a good one. You have both believed où je n'étais pas sure/ where I was not sure. It's so important when one doesn't have the needed conviction that someone else has it--- Merci Normand! It's been damn necessary!!!"

Micheline then tells me that her mother had called her about some photos and that she was apparently in tears. [My parents] truly suffer and it's tragic, she says. "Quelle vie gaspillée---what a wasted life. I may have a hard time pulling my life together, mais je ne veux pas gaspiller ce bien si précieux qui est la vie--but I don't want to ruin this gift so precious that is life. That's why I must confront my apprehensions & continue, continue!" Then she asks me about the publisher Plon who had contacted me about my novel that I was writing. I had a possible interview set up by a secretary that never materialized, and Micheline was with me in Paris when I told her about the interview. She told me that was good news when a publisher invites you over. It never happened. I was lied to by the secretary and the interview with the publisher simply melted away. My dream of being published by a Paris publisher was shattered that day. The secretary was more interested in my being an American and living in the States where she wanted to go some day than eager to connect me with her boss. Apparently she fabricated the interview with a Monsieur Jean Malaurie who was leaving soon for the Orient and I was left in the lurch. I was naïve then and so terribly sure that things were coming to fruition as far as my writing was concerned. I forgot Plon and never tried to find a Paris publisher again. I tried the Québécois venues instead. Over the years I always sent Micheline a copy of my recent book and she always promised to read it on the train to Annecy or Grenoble or wherever she was headed. She promised me some analysis of each book I sent her but never did it. I would have liked her thoughts on my works since she was so analytically qualified and sharp when it comes to analyzing thoughts on paper. I suppose she was always busy with her art and preoccupied with her finances. I never pressed her for her analyses. That is why we planned to have a summer workshop in Varengeville where both of us would participate, each one with our creativity and our thoughts on producing works of art, me with words her with watercolors and oils. Unfortunately it never came to fruition. I'm sorry now that I did not pursue this venture. Micheline must have thought that I had abandoned this project since she never mentioned it afterwards. I sincerely believe that would have been a collective exercise in teaching and producing creative results. Moreover, such a workshop would have encouraged Micheline to anchor herself in not so troubled waters and have more confidence in herself as a person and as an artist. She truly needed a fellow artist to be with her in her teaching. And I believe I would have learned from her and she from me. Man/woman proposes and God disposes, is the adage I believe in.

As I have already said, Micheline was always concerned about the publication of my books and in March of 1994 she went to the "Salon du Livre" in Paris in order to procure for me some literature about being published in France. She then says that her stage/course in Sologne was filling up with 18 students in all three weeks. She tells me that she would be more than thrilled if we could share a course together. She urged me to work seriously on this venture. She then talks about my one-woman play called "La Souillonne." It's about a retired millworker who tells her story and it's written in colloquial French or our dialect. She gave the book to her daughter Monique whose reaction was to tell me that I ought to consider some type of television story, but that only in France would it be appreciated. Then she adds, "Don't forget the importance of visual imagery!" That's the imaginative Micheline Bousquet, the creative artist.

In her letter dated October 1st, 1994, Micheline writes that she has thought it out and says, "faire confiance à ses sensations et ses profondes indications"/---to rely on one's sensations and profound indications---was a hard lesson but worthwhile and terribly important. "As a result," she states, "I have changed my approach and I am convinced that I should write something about creativity." She doesn't want to emprison herself mentally and even emotionally. She desires the freedom to create. She tells me that she has maintained teaching the plastic arts because she does have the know-how in this realm and is unusual & able to demystify art and its language désacraliser/take away its sacred aura---"symbolism is universal and governs by some issues or facts that we find universally and intimately tied to nature if one knows how to observe nature. For students who wish to deepen their well-being, their vitality, their courage, their creativity, in all their capacity to live, I started a workshop on VITALITÉ ET ÉNERGIE INTÉRIEURE ---and it's already full." She ends the letter by again urging me to put together a workshop that I will present with her in Varengeville. Unfortunately, it did not happen due to my hesitation and lack of determination to leave home and go to France leaving my family alone and wondering what I was doing. J'étais lâche, indécis et tout probablement peureux d'avoir à m'affranchir de mon devoir familial culturel franco-Américain/I was lazy, undecided and most probably fearful of having to free myself from my Franco-American cultural sense of duty. It's truly a harness thrown upon your shoulders when you are born in that particular culture. God free us from slavery and indecision. That harness turns to become a burden with time. Anyway, I never did offer that workshop that I would have so terribly loved. Besides, it would have done some good for my dearest friend Micheline, the artist, in soul, heart and body. She so needed support in any way in any venues it might come. Quite often it was not there. So, she struggled until she became stressed out to the point of depression and fear of not being accepted by those she respected and counted on. I could see the spiral of self-destruction spinning and spinning downward. Where was the good fortune of financial success and celebratory recognition by those who are in the know and who admit creative artists in their midst. Where were they, and how does one get to achieve success and earn enough money to live a healthy and generous life. Yes, where were they. Where are they now. Creativity can be easily restored if we all support the least of artistic endeavors by a talented and committed one who shows promise of true creativity. That was Micheline Bousquet's dream, as a doer and teacher.

In the meantime, what was happening in the family? How were the two daughters doing. Were they affected by their mother's life and pursuit of creativity? How did they manage the lack of money that certainly affected the mother? Did they complain about being "poor"? How did they cope with a mother who was absent from home a lot of times? How did they adjust to French customs, language, society, school, and many other challenges that were foisted on them since their arrival in France? These are some of the questions that I felt needed to be answered in some fashion. In the following chapter I will attempt to answer these question the best I can.

CHAPTER THREE:

LA VIE FAMILALE DES BOUSQUET EN FRANCE/FAMILY LIFE OF THE BOUSQUETS IN FRANCE

AS I HAVE said before, one of the core values of Franco-American life is family. I do not know if Micheline Bousquet's two daughters can be deemed as being Franco-American. The mother certainly was but the father was not. The only thing I know about him is that his first name is John and his last place of residence was Delaware. That's all I know about him. He did not speak French neither did the two daughters at first. Did Micheline raise them with Franco-American values. I doubt it. Did the maternal grandparents have any influence on them? I really do not know except that the two girls hardly ever saw their grandparents and Micheline kept them afar from them since she had bad memories of what she called the "tragic life" of both her parents. She remembers growing up with negative vibes, a lack of love and intimacy and a desire on the part of the parents to send her away so that Micheline could be disciplined into a well-behaved, obedient child and not an excitée. Did Micheline ever reject her cultural roots as a Franco-American? No, and she did not reject her maternal language which is French. She eventually found out that her maternal language served her well as a person and a creative artist in a country whose language was French.

How did the two daughters, Mia and Monique, adjust to a move like that? Moving to France. Micheline once told me that both her daughters adjusted extremely well and learned the French language very easily by immersion and close contact with the French population. Children can very easily learn and adapt to cultural values. Language is one of the instruments of adaptation in a foreign country. Micheline had the basics of French since childhood and I'm sure she learned how to deepen and polish her French while teaching her daughters how to speak their new tongue. If you throw someone in the water he/she learns how to swim. That's how Mia and Monique learned French, customs, ways of communication and the idioms that are thrown at you without realizing that they become part of your speech. As far as I know, Mia and Monique never complained about such learning experiences in what was for them an entirely foreign experience. They learned to follow the mother in whatever way they were given without any question without any recalcitrancy. They were good daughters. But they could not be classified as Franco-Americans. However, one cannot say that there were no influences on the part of the mother whose name was French, BOUSQUET. There must have been some remnants of that heritage left in Micheline's blood, gestures, customs, and values. One cannot erase completely those cultural affinities. Besides, a mother is a mother and mothers do pass on certain values and certain ways of communicating and expressing oneself.

Just how did Mia and Monique fare in a society that seems strange and foreign,? First of all, they were but young children and young children adapt easily under the motherly watchful gaze and the comfort of the mother's wings ever prudent and caring. Gradually Micheline tried to teach her daughters how to become more and more independent, meaning learning to be, think and act on your own without being cast away from the loving gaze of the mother/caretaker and all the while casting her influence as an artist, especially a creative one. Micheline just did not want to be like her mother, non-flexible, hard-driven by a set of religious and cultural values and especially unwavering in her thoughts and ideas about raising a child. Everyone conforms, everyone admits no faults in their comportment and no one waivers from a lack of respect for parental guidance. And, especially no one, as a child, plays the role of an excitée, a wild and disrespectful one. Micheline did not adhere to these values and she even felt scathed by them. Her growing-up was not the best of her younger years.

As I read her letters and my notes, I discover that Micheline is drawing closer and closer to her own publicity as well as some marketing but she is not doing so well in the marketing phase. She never was good at it due to a lack of marketing knowledge and most probably skills. She does have some skills in thinking out loud and is very skillful at coming out with new ways and new venues for the exibition of her art work. Her cheery personality opens her up to contacts and people who recognize her creativity and friendly and warm demeanor. However, warmth and pleasurable charm do not sell paintings.

On October first 1998, I received a brief letter from her in which was enclosed a brochure entitled "Espace Saint-Antoine." The information reads as follows: "L'Espace Saint-Antoine ni galerie, ni dépôt-vente, mais un alternatif offert aux artistes et au public. L'art n'est pas toujours un coup de coeur, mais un apprivoisement. L'art est instinctif et parfois il faut provoquer l'explosion des barrières qui nous empêchent de voir et de recevoir.

L'artiste dans ce projet est appelé à un engagement de temps et un investissement de sa part pour permettre à son oeuvre d'être vue et re-vue. Il doit être partant pour ne plus confondre la valeur artistique avec la valeur marchande afin de pratiquer des prix pour un large public.

Pour le public ce lieu de vie est ouvert à tous. Il peut venir pour le plaisir de l'oeil, le plaisir de rencontrer ou le plaisir d'une contemplation silencieuse. S'il souhaite acquérir une oeuvre, tout sera fait pour que cela soit possible et devienne un acte de joie et satisfaction.

Micheline Bousquet est par ailleurs consultante en ressource humaine dans un travail de "coaching" de dirigeante , de cadres, professions libérales, projets associatifs et individuels.

As a kind of footnote, "Le coaching est une opportunité pour l'individu de: mieux affirmer ses perceptions, la manière dont il mobilise ses ressources, prépare ses décisions, s'authorise à agir ou non.

---accélérer la prise de conscience de ses angles morts

---agir autrement avec ce qu'il est.

---découvrir et favoriser une efficacité constamment renouvelée.

---développer sa satisfaction au quotidien

Translation: Espace Saint-Antoine neither gallery, nor sales-depot, but an alternative offered to artists and the public. Art is not always a heartfelt attempt but a taming. Art is instinctive and sometimes one must provoke the explosion of the barriers that prevent us to see and receive. The artist in this project is called to an engagement of time and investment on his part to allow his work to be seen and re-seen. He has to be well-spoken so that the artistic value is not to be confused with the selling value so as to set prices. As for the public, this locale of life is opened to everyone. One can come for the pleasure of the eye, the pleasure of meeting someone or the pleasure of a silent contemplation. If one wishes to buy a work of art, everything will be done so that everything will be made possible and become an act of joy and satisfaction. Micheline Bousquet is furthermore a consultant in human resources in the work of coaching, of leadership, administrator, liberal professions, associate or individual projects.---coaching is an opportunity for individuals to   a) better refine his perceptions, the way he mobilizes his resources, prepare his decisions, authorizes himself to act or not;   b) accelerate his awareness of his blind spots,   c) act otherwise with who he is   d) discover and favorize an efficacity constantly revealed,   d) develop his satisfaction daily.

There were many things that confirmed Micheline's separation from her mother but one that finally resolved the problem of distance in miles and relationship. When her father died he left everything to her mother and when she passed away she hardly left anything to Micheline, barely the trifle sum of 10%. Most of the inheritance went to the brother. Nothing to the two grandchildren, Mia and Monique. That's what troubled Micheline if it did not completely affirm the fact that her mother practically disowned Micheline and completely rejected the two granddaughters as not being of her own blood. That's what affected Micheline's sense of belonging. She had longed for family ties to be mended and her daughters united to the Bousquet lineage, so she thought. However, death only brought or rather confirmed disunity. Her mother confirmed the cutting off of any relationship with Micheline and her own family. To her death, Micheline's mother, Rita Samson Bousquet, denied any relationship with her granddaughters and that's what affected Micheline's deep emotions regarding grandmother and granddaughters. She would rather have no inheritance and see that any amount of money be given to Mia and Monique confirming some family acceptance on the part of the grandmother. But it never came and Micheline was deeply hurt. Micheline, cared enough to express her hurt feelings. She called it monstrous on the part of her mother. Micheline had to live with it and carried it for as long as she lived. That affected her sense of belonging and her sense of sensibility.

Micheline moved from Varengeville to Nantes in early August 2000. However, she did not let go of her "home" in Varengeville. That was her pied à terre as they say, her domicile. In her letter dated September 25th, she talks about her conference on "coaching", éthique/pratique, she calls it. She tells me that it was a difficult one but once she began it went really well. It was her first conference on the subject. However, she admits that she misses painting and that she will find time to do art work again. "I'm not able to do both," she says, "I've tried and c'est pas possible."

Micheline adds in that letter, "How I wish I could just sit & talk with you face to face...comme tu as constaté pendant toutes ces années,"/ as you have noticed during all these years, "that writing is not my forté. You are one of the very few, si pas le seul vraiment, if not truly the only one, I can talk to freely and you listen." Then she continues by saying, "I have passed your écriture/writing to someone in Paris who apparently knows or who has a connexion to Bernard Pivot "Bouillon de Culture"... we'll see what develops." She then adds that she had heard the rumor that this was his last year of his broadcasting and that she was going to let me know later on. Personally I had heard of Bernard Pivot and his acclaimed personality as a radio host but nothing came out of Micheline's contact. I never received word either from Bernard Pivot or his network. I'm sure I was somewhat of a lost soul as an author in all of the Francophone world. I wasn't a known subject in the land of a Bernard Pivot's cultural plan. J'étais plutôt à la dérive des eaux littéraires/ I was rather adrift in the literary waters, I would say.

"It seems strange for me to be living what I am living through, the work I'm doing," Micheline writes, "La reconnaissance/recognition is something so new...ça ne me monte pas à la tête...c'est simplement pour moi quelque chose so unknown until now./it doesn't go to my head...it's simply for me something so unknown. It's recognition for what I think, what I feel, what I'm able to accomplish...ça fait tout drôle en tout cas"/it's totally funny in any case. This is precisely what she has been seeking most of her life, recognition by family, by friends and by believers in art and creativity. It has been a rough road for Micheline Bousquet, rough because the road to success has been bumpy and full of curves, not at all smooth. Except for her daughters, those closest to her made the journey on that road difficult and at times perilous to her sense of psychological safety and assurance. Nothing is so perilous as recrimination and lack of support in the handling of the creative soul as that of Micheline, the artist.

Micheline adds, "I hope that the Bousquets have not tried to contact you again to find out about me...I'm truly sorry to have to ask you not to share with anyone of them anything about me, but it's very important that I remain untouchable. I'm still working in psychotherapy and I'm slowly being brought to realize where I've come from, à quoi j'ai échappé/what I have escaped...and the need for protection from them." It's truly sad to realize that Micheline's family members are the culprits in her lack of trust and lack of love. She then closes the letter by asking me to send her a small box of fall leaves. Fallen but alive with color and unbroken memories. The fallen autumn leaves of New England. Color, color for Micheline is somewhat of a blessing that soothes the memory of happier days. .

After Nantes came a return to Varengeville and a Christmas card wishing me the best and reminding me of the close friendship we share with some of the happy memories such as the new fallen snow, the blueberry pie that I had made as well as the piece left in the kitchen and stolen by the huge and spoiled dog, Boris, that made us laugh. Micheline loved that animal 'til his death a few years later.

Next came a letter apprising me of a video that had just been made that publicized Micheline's works of art. She wanted me to send her my honest opinions of the video once I saw it. (I never got it). However, worse than that was a cry of desperation, a desperation for money since she found herself in serious debt. Micheline had that weakness, spending money she did not have. If she felt the need to get something be it expensive brushes, oil paints, canvases or a necessity to spend on some worthwhile publicity she felt so strongly about but could not afford, she went ahead and purchased the product even if she knew she hadn't the money but relied on loans or possible sales of her work for future income. But now she tells me that she is desperate. "I'm hauling my rear-end to try to get through this time period which I feel is the most difficult because I know the project will work and open doors," she writes. Reading this letter made me sense the desperation and pleading. Then she tells me that Monique has taken her mother's pressbook to Lyon with her and tried to interest some galleries in Micheline's works. All of them are enthusiastically interested and it shows promise on their part, but no commitment. Micheline talks of future exhibits in Nantes, Clisson, and, of course, Lyon. But the problem is now, she states, can she cope with the present problem of finances. She begs for my help in reaching out to possible loaners since she says, "My dignity would hold up better if this was repayment or exchange---les dons sont encore difficiles pour moi d'accepter/gifts are still difficult for me to accept." SOS are her last words. I tried to do whatever I could but with small results. My own finances were meager at that time. My heart sank at the thought that I failed her.

The next letter written January 24, 2000, is Micheline's brief but meaningful analyses of some of my books that I mailed to her over the months. She always promises me to read them and send me her thoughts on whatever she read. This time she gives me her comments on three books, one a biographical novel Le Petit Mangeur de Coeurs-Saignants, a second one a novel based on the story of my maternal grandmother and my mother, "Deux Femmes, Deux Rêves, and a third one, tales and legends, Lumineau. This last one has several tales and some legends and Micheline analyzes all of them telling me which ones are her favorites. She names "la Bonnefemme aux Chats" about a woman who so loved cats that one day she turned into one is one of her favorites. I had written this one based on MIcheline's serious love for cats. Of course, there was her love for Boris the big dog. She found "L'Arbre crochu" superbe, and loved the ending. I had written this one based on a small tree that I planted in my front yard given to me by a neighbor. It was indeed crooked, but I planted it anyway. In the story, the man who plants it is deformed and is considered crooked but at the end of the tale he stands upright like the tree that changes and grows upright and tall. All of the tales and legends were accompanied with a drawing by a friend of mine, Shelley Schoenberg, whom I commissioned to make each one according to my wishes and the meaning of each work. He did an excellent job. All one has to do is pick up a copy of LUMINEAU and examine the artwork. It's excellent and creative. I like the one dealing with the legend of Squando and the Saco River. Shelley Schoenberg is truly an artist and teacher. He now lives somewhere out west with his daughter, I believe.

Then Micheline advises me that I shouldn't rely strictly on the demands of publishers especially in Montreal and Paris, and that I should look into the Swiss publishers as well as the Belgian ones for my French works. I did but without success. Also, she tells me to adhere to my maternal tongue which is French but moreover I should write in the Franco-American dialect since it comes not only from the heart but the soul. Of course, Micheline relates all of this to her favorite theme of creativity. You need to be yourself, your very own being when you create, she tells me. Eventually I did write in our dialect. I wrote two plays, La Souillonne, and La Souillonne Deusse and I am presently finishing writing another one in our dialect, La Souillonne et son cat'chisse en images. This dialect is a verbal/oral communication that I learned growing up. It was the family and the entire neighborhood tongue. Nothing in writing, no lexicons, no dictionary so that when I write in the dialect, it comes from my memory, my heart and my soul experiences. Micheline understood that very well. She asks the question, "Ça tu du bon sens vouloir écrire dans sa langue maternelle"/ Does it make sense to write in your maternal language? Then she answers, "You bet your damn ass it does!!! Why---parce que c'est le langage de ton âme"/it's the language of your soul, she insists. She continues, "What makes the writing extra authentic is its language---take Color Purple---it's tough reading if you aren't a Black American---but it just wouldn't have the strength it does have without it being written as it was." She goes on to say that publishers should not refuse to publish works in the dialect and that refusal means it's an excuse on their part, and "doesn't cut it for

me." Let's just say that Micheline truly understood and practiced creativity artistically and she understood me as a writer. And, I understood her and her dilemma of a woman troubled by family matters but willing to sacrifice relationships for the sake of authentic creativity. For Micheline, the soul speaks and not the tongue, the heart is in harmony with the soul so that the two of them fly above the nets of ethnic values as well as the so-called professional values and the artist is thus liberated from exigencies and barriers in his/her artistic creative expression. That's the language and thoughts of a Stephen Daedalus in Portrait of An Artist As A Young Man. To fly over the nets of ethnicity. I've always captured this thought and feeling as my own in reading and re-reading James Joyce's classic. I've often made Stephen Daedalus's declaration as mine in the secret of my heart.

After a long hiatus, Micheline resumed writing to me. In her letter dated March 30, 1986, she tells me that she is fighting a tension, an anxiety within herself, "une tension psychique qui monte à des proportions radicales à l'intérieur de moi chaque fois qu'une chance se présente pour faire connaître mon travail...et je capitule---je deviens incapable d'aller au bout de mon désir---j'ai un vrai et fort désir d'exister---je prends le grand risque de faire de la peinture qui demande le regard de l'autre(pas l'acceptation ni l'amour que le regard) mais ce regard je le fuis...je le soupçonne. Drôle de drame...mais cela est mon drame. C'est une origine compliquée---et nous mettons pas facilement de côté le manque d'exister...d'être regardé comme il le fallait par la première qui nous donne son regard...la mère...my mother has succeeded in passing to all 3 of her children her pathology...quite unconsciously but most surely."/a psychic tension that goes up to radical proportions in the interior of myself each time that a chance presents itself to make my work known....and I capitulate....I become incapable of going to the end of my desire---I have a true and strong desire of existing---I take the great risk of doing some painting that demands the look of the other(not the acceptance nor the love) but the look that I flee from..I suspect it. Strange drama. It's a complicated origin---and we do not easily put aside the lack of existence...to be looked at like it had to be by the first one who gives us her look...the mother.

"So I started since last June," she says, "to take si je veux être/if I want to be...extremely difficult for me, but I have to do it...find exhibit places right here in Varengeville..the strange and curious beast has come out of her hiding place...and I have started another expo at Saint-Valéry-en-Caux. I have a lot of work to do," she says.

Micheline explains her difficulties especially that of emotional stress, "I've always held back my deep emotional expression in my work and even camouflaged it in part by a very abstract intellectual expression & every once in a while something came to the surface that was extremely powerful... since I'm still doing some non-figurative work & more expressive work & even have titled much of it...so far I consider this my best work but no longer "marchandable" pour mettre sur tes murs sauf si vraiment 'l'art est une nécessité'. Je ne peux pas me compromettre... si je veux être regardé... je dois être regardé en authenticité...et une partie de cela inclus mon mal de vivre."/ salable to put on your walls except truly 'art is a necessity'. I cannot compromise myself...if I want to be looked at...I must be looked at in authenticity... and part of that includes my pain of living.

Micheline tells me that she made a friend, a Mary G. whose husband worked in the pharmaceuticals and was spending time with Rhone-Poulenc Meriaux in Paris. She has been working with Mary in her courses for five years but now the husband's time is up and they must go back to the States. Mary tells Micheline that she, the artist of creativity, builds bridges for people to define and come in contact with their own creativity. Micheline says that she intuitively gets people to discover from a feeling point of view how they can motivate themselves "(amazing we always teach what we most often need to learn ourselves!!! I think my own difficulties make my work credible. Because of my own suffering that I creatively transform to teach others, I close the distance between 'le maître et l'élève'/master and student, and this is very important if a message is to pass, be heard, transformed as the individual needs it to be."

Micheline ends by saying the "ménage se porte bien"/the menagerie is well. That Boris is still alive and that she now has six cats."Oui, c'est ma folie et ma vie/it's my foolishness and my life" she declares. So much for the love and caring she carries in her heart, I say.

The next mail I received from Micheline was not a letter but an entire syllabus of a new course : ATELIER DE CRÉATIVITÉ ***Stages de Printemps---L'EXPÉRIENCE CRÉATIVE : L'AQUARELLE avec MICHELINE BOUSQUET . This was being offered in three stages--- April and early May. Included in the syllabus is a short introduction where she states: "Ce n'est peut-être pas un choix de devenir peintre, on l'est... tout doucement...mais choisir la France pour s'exprimer dans ce métier est comme un retour aux sources. J'ai compris en tant qu'aquarelliste le très peu d'importance donnée à l'aquarelle comme une forme d'art pur et les idées fausses que les gens possèdent envers ce médium et forme d'expression."/ It's probably not a choice of becoming a painter, we are...very softly... but to choose France in order to express oneself in this craft is like a return to the sources. I have understood as a watercolorist the very little importance given to watercolor as a form of pure art and the false ideas that people possess towards this medium and form of expression. All in all, it's a very detailed syllabus with the registration form and the needs that are required of the incoming students such as brushes, colors, paper, ARCHE 300 gm. grain TORCHON, toothbrushes, Bocassan no.20, and sponges. The course was being offered by the co-partnership of Micheline Bousquet and Claudette Poccioli. It sounded like a very interesting discovery for students in need of an artistic adventure as well as a teacher in need of a creative challenge. Micheline also mentions that there will be six other courses given: Bandol, St-Germain-en-Laye, Annecy, la Normandie, la Bretagne, and the southwest. Quite a challenge and a proposal of fine arts specifically watercolor. Micheline seemed to be in the thick of it, that is, fighting for her artistic life and working hard at being creative while developing her skills at being a publicist and a marketing agent. She was doing her best to stay afloat financially speaking. I do not know how all of this turned out. All I know is that she truly put her heart and soul into this project.

The next letter dated Friday evening, Februay 27 1987, Micheline has just returned home in Varengeville. She flew from Nice. She had just terminated her workshops on l'Aquarelle, four and a half days, she says. "It went extremely well," she insists, and she is looking forward to the other workshops already planned. If this materializes, she adds, it will mean a wonderful adventure and will give her some financial stability as well as providing contacts and general public awareness of her work, not as a teacher but as an aquarelliste. "I believe I have an ability to communicate my passion" she tells me, "and the evaluations have been so good you wouldn't believe...and my workshops have evolved because of my students." Then she lists several comments, the best of them being, 'you give openly, focusing always on the positive...and how to change problems on a painting with opportunities.'" She goes on to say, "Norman, I'm absolutely shocked with pleasure...I don't know or didn't know these dimensions. I with your help...Ben/Janine...Mme Roche, I'm beginning for the first time in 40 years to believe I may have some magic too. It will never be able to go to my head because I've been so buried under and coming to the Vézinet, being or trying to be eaten up by Mme Tamboise who really débarrasse/gets rid of --Marie, Nelly sur moi à chaque moment et prend toute mon énergie vitale...je dis stop!! non...pour la première fois je dis NON. Je me secoue parce que quand on est si diminué il y qu'à remonter...rien à perdre sauf gagner la vie---ou on abandonne complètement et, merde, je n'ai pas venu jusqu'ici pour être enterrerée. Ça viendra beaucoup trop vite/who really gets rid of Marie, Nelly away from me every moment and it takes all of my vital energy...I say stop! no for the first time, I say NO. I shake myself off because when we are diminished there's only to climb back...nothing to lose except to win over life---or we abandon completely and, shit, I did not come up to here to be buried in the ground. That will come much too fast--- me I want to live---but I'm tired of scraping by---I've got talent & now I can even communicate and get people to believe they too have have their special magic---true they won't all be Picassos nor even Bousquets but each has the potential for individual expression & must investigate it, develop it!" These words of self-encouragement and purposeful determination on her part are a new awakening. She would have had to develop this awakening a long time ago in order to shake off the maternal psychotic infractions. I'm not a psychiatrist; I don't know. But I do know that a child be it five or forty years old needs love and encouragement. Not rejection. Rejection hurts.

Le Vézinet was a commune in the Yvelines department in the Île-de-France. It was part of the affluent suburbs of western Paris. It was known for its wooded avenues, mansions and lakes. Micheline was occasionally invited there to present her workshops. She found the participants somewhat snobbish and not very cooperative with her instructions. But it meant money for her.

If workshops and conferences help out and if one is determined to get the most out of them, then I say go for it. These venues helped Micheline to come in contact with people and establish a network of friends who encouraged her to blossom and to become fruitful in many ways. Sure, she was the artist but she needed others, others to look at her as an artist and her art as well as believe in her talent that she truly had. Her family, the men in her life never offered her any consolation nor any love. They all made her feel diminished and not worth the effort. She did not thrive, she withered instead. It took an awful lot of convincing to make her feel wanted and to get her started on her career as a creative artist. The only terrible difficulty was the finances which she could never overcome. She wrestled with them and did not learn how to market herself and her artworks. She did try very hard to learn how to do it but never quite succeeded. It was a never ending struggle. But she did try and try very very hard. I give her an A+ for trying.

CHAPTER FOUR :

LES AMIS

ONE THING FOR sure, if there had not been friends in Micheline's life her career as an artist would have suffered tremendously. That's what I believe. I may be wrong but I sense that the lack of human contact and friendship would have diminished her ability to reach out and even flourish in her own time and space. Les amis are not only important but I dare say, vital. Vital means vitality and vitality connotes life. What Micheline means when she says "Fais pas ton excitée!" on the part of her mother, meant to her, stop living. I can understand that. So eventually friends filled in the tremendous gap that had been carved in Micheline's life. She needed gaps, holes, huge emptinesses to be filled with warmth and good feelings of amitié, tendres amitiés. It took a long time coming but it did especially with the presence of her two daughters, Monique and Mia. They became the core of friendship and friendly survival for her. Micheline's father Jean, her mother Rita, her brother John and her sister, did not ever SOS fill those gaps and holes. Rather they widened them and left them empty. Micheline realized that even when she was a young girl. It persisted throughout her lifetime.

I do not know anything about friendship during her college years. Micheline never talked about them as if they had not existed. They did exist since she went to one undergraduate college and one graduate college and came out with a graduate degree in Human Development. She did not follow up on this path since she was convinced by an art professor to make her art talent and experience her possible calling in life. At one point, Micheline became disenchanted with her studies and what she had learned in college as well as her job opportunities with handicapped children. I suppose it was not meant for her. She became particularly morose at the thought of becoming a failure in life. Besides, as she says, she had two children to take care of and they took much of her precious time with very litle time on her hands to pursue artistic ventures. However, a good friend became her fairy godmother as luck and friendship would have it. She then decided after her divorce to plunge into creative arts at the bidding of a close friend who saw the need to enliven Micheline by giving her some art supplies just to get her energized and give her a chance to realize that she, Micheline Bousquet, had talent for creative art.

I'm sure she made friends with certain people during her years of wandering and thinking about her future. She never talked to me about it. However, Micheline did encounter some dear friends as early as her first encounter with one of the two ladies in St-Jean-Cap-Ferrat, Madame Roche. Madame Roche was a widow living with her sister. They owned the property where Micheline and her daughters first lived in France. Micheline soon discovered that Madame Roche was the warm and friendly one. She also was the one who was able to plumb Micheline's talent as an artist. She's the one who told Micheline that her talent came from her tripes/bowels, travelled through her head and went right straight through her fingers. That was the kind of metaphor she used and Micheline recognized that it was true. Her creative drive came from her bowels and it was forceful. From the depths of her bold incarnation of ideas, imagined designs and striking colors came forth to stir up creative concepts that went up to her head where the cerebral, cognitive and artistic energies interconnected and then passed on the results to her manipulative and able fingers that handled creatively and skilfully the watercolors and the oils to render them into works of art. That was Madame Roche's interpretation of Micheline's skills as an artist. Micheline loved Madame Roche and so did the kids. There was an occasion later on when Monique had grown up that Madame Veuve J.B. Roche sponsored an exhibit of Micheline's oil paintings and watercolors along with Monique's ceramics. It was held in the garden of the Villa la Rocheraie in St-Jean-Cap-Ferrat at the residence of Colonel Jean-Baptiste Roche, husband of the widow Madame Roche. Apparently Monique had grown into her own and was ready to demonstrate her skills as an artist alongside her mother. Both Monique and Mia were the essence and core of the love that formed the true Bousquet family that Micheline so desired and nurtured.

Then there was Ben and Janine, the loveable couple who lived in Nice and travelled to Monaco for daily work. That's where Micheline met them in Monaco at the Oceanographic Museum. Micheline did some translation. The couple found Monique and Mia loveable and sweet. The girls soon adopted them as close friends and companions. Micheline relied on Ben and Janine for counsel and help. She and her daughters were often invited to their apartment in Nice. Friendship flourished and Micheline soon felt wanted and accepted as a close friend. They became the family that Micheline never really had. If there were difficulties that Micheline had to face, she went to Ben and Janine for help.

One very good example of this is the time Micheline was practically thrown out of her dwelling place in St-Jean-Cap-Ferrat. There had been somewhat of a quarrel between Madame Roche's sister and Micheline. It wasn't really a quarrel but a misunderstanding and the old lady had hit Micheline hard. Micheline could not take that and decided to move away from there. So in came Ben and Janine who offered Micheline and her daughters a temporary dwelling place at their apartment. That was about the time I was on my way to visit Micheline. I've already mentioned the details of my getting there and finding Micheline gone. I spent the night in a neighboring room offered to me by a gentle innskeeper. Well, it so happened that both Ben and Janine offered to lodge me at their home for a week or so. They were both so very accueillants/welcoming. I stayed with them and enjoyed their company. It was there and at that time that I gave Micheline her first recorded interview with me. All of us travelled together and visited some delightful places. When I found out that it was Ben's birthday, I bought him a cake on my way back to the apartment. The three of them had been working all day in Monaco and the girls were in school. When I left to fly home, Ben and Janine knew I liked santons/little clay saints for Christmas, they gave me three of them as a souvenir. They were such warm, delighful and loving people. I will never forget them. I did buy and sent them university sweatshirts that they enjoyed very much. A present from a close friend.

Then there were contacts that Micheline established in her many trips throughout France some of which became friends such as Mary G, an older American student of hers living in Paris while her husband was doing a practicum for some pharmaceutical company. The two of them spent many a weekend working on plans for future workshops. Micheline needed the relationship and cooperation that were splendidly established. Her feelings and creativity seemed to flourish with the presence of Mary G.

Furthermore, there's the people who helped Micheline with her workshops such as Claudette Poccioli of Nice who worked tirelessly trying to establish worthwhile publicity for Micheline's several workshops. Then there was Micheline's teaming up with other artists that could easily be matched with her own talent for public production. She had a knack of finding artists who needed not only contacts but venues to exhibit their art. Among them, Pierre Rescan, a musicothérapeute who explored sounds and odors within the context of art forms such as paintings and music. Then there was Anne Lemaire, an artist that Micheline truly respected for her sense of color and her state of "presence" in her creativity; the sculptor Bozo, born in Nantes, whose works concentrate on the notion of l'Arbre/the tree. whose wood becomes the living element of artistry in the able hands of one who calls himself Bozo. Micheline recognized in

Bozo an artist of quality in his creative endeavors. With Bozo the sculptor, Micheline adheres to her conviction of art for creative sake, a belief that draws to her so many artists like Bozo that are drawn to her and desire to be linked to her creativity and sense of being alive in a world of many art forms be it painting, watercolor, music, dance or even wood. Nothing is excluded from Micheline's list of artistic composition and venues. You can easily mix and match various talents and artistic products so that the mind and heart and soul can be in harmony with whatever is deemed creative according to Micheline Bousquet.

Micheline respected and praised my work on Adelard Coté, a local folk sculptor and farmer born in Quebec, emigrated to New England and eventually became a wood sculptor because his wife, Eva, inspired him, no, incited him to fill his winter hours with the sculpting of horses in wood. Since he was also a forgeron/ blacksmith, he worked with metal and leather to duplicate the harnesses, saddles, spurs and chain links that he used with his sculptures. He did not do it for money not even fame but for his own enjoyment and his pride in succeeding in the production of so many fascinating wood sculptures. This was my very first book. It was written both in French and in English. The book includes several photos of Coté's sculptures taken by the master photographer, Stephen Muskie, masters degree from the Rochester Institute of Technology. Micheline considered the folk artist as being creative and down-to-earth while she admired me for my talent as a developing writer who struggled with the search for publication. That's a very difficult part of writing and getting known. Publishers are not easy to reach and especially to be accepting of a writer's work. One has to be creative in the craft of writing and creative in the skills of finding a publisher. Micheline understood that very well. The book is entitled, L'Enclume et le Couteau---The Life and Work of Adelard Coté, Folk Artist/The Anvil and the Carving Knife.

I had agreed to send Micheline everything I would write in the course of my writing days.(Over the years I sent her every book I wrote both in

French and in English). I had started writing for publication(at least I was hoping for publication) a few years before I retired from teaching at the university. I loved teaching and I did not want to leave early. However, there came a time when I had had it with students who refrained from reading the given assignments and even refused to buy the necessary books prescribed. I could not believe it. Besides, some of them had a hard time reading. I believe that they graduated from high school with a reading level of the 5th or 6th grade if not lower. No wonder they did not like to read. I taught literature and that requires reading skills. Towards the end of my teaching career at the University of New England, I designed a course entitled "The Solitary Hero: Jean Valjean, Étienne Lantier and Tom Joad." The students had to read Hugo's Les Misérables(a sort of abridged version), Zola's Germinal and Steinbeck's Grapes of Wrath. The course included some visual aids such as the movies based on each novel. All intrinsinctly linked to full discussions and theme-related in-class presentations by students. ONE student, Maureen M. who was a humanities student adhered closely to the syllabus and read every assigned reading. Most of the other twenty or so students were physical therapy or occupationl therapy students. They were the ones who were not doing the readings or who borrowed the books from each other but failed to complete the prescribed readings. Therefore, class discusssions were short, unenlightened and deprived of meaningful topics based on characters and plot. I did what I had told myself I would not do, lecture most of the time. Maureen did very well in the course while most of the others struggled in order to get a decent grade and a desired GPA. It was indeed a failed attempt on my part to educate young people in the realm of classical literature. I was beginning to think that many of those students, although quite intelligent, had never read a complete novel. That's when I decided to retire from teaching early. That was also an opportunity for me to write although I had started writing my first novel while carrying a full teaching load. At one point, I was even the chair of the Department of the Humanities. The teaching load as well as the administrative duties kept me ever so busy. However, I did it and enjoyed it. Teaching is a work of dedication and trust. Trust that the teacher is a dedicated artisan who knows how to stimulate students and shows them the way in becoming educated persons of learning. Teaching and learning are not only for the degree but especially for the formation of the mind and soul. Otherwise it would be just an exercise in reading books and writing papers with a grade attached to it. Micheline Bousquet was a true and dedicated teacher. She knew how to meet the many challenges of teaching and artful endeavors. She was indeed a master artist.

That is why and when Micheline started being quite interested in my attempts at writing books and getting published. The teacher in her would not allow her to omit my work as a writer. I had had long discussions with her about my being serious about writing and she always tried to encourage me to follow my desire and abilities to write my stories. However, I hesitated putting stories into words because I did not think I could do it and do it well. Besides, I did not know if I should do it in English or in French. I knew I had the ability to do both. I had been teaching French for close to thirty years. But, how does one get started? I had read that St-Exupéry had said once that the best way to get going is to write about personal experiences. What we know best. So, I decided to write my first novel about the family, both sides, the Huberts and the Beauprés while changing some names so that no one would be offended if I should mention something that didn't go well with anyone. I decided to call it, Au fil de l'eau, with a reference to the Saco River and the mills in our stretch of the land. It would be in French since I knew I could do it, in correct, acceptable and standard French. I had in mind of writing an epic of the French-Canadians who emigrated to New England in the 19th Century and at the beginning of the 20th. That would include both sides of my extended family. With time, I recognized all the work I would have to do in writing an epic. I wasn't prepared for that. So, I decided to write about myself, since I knew myself best. I would write about my growing up. I would keep the family stories for later on. My growing up story would be in French and its title would be "Le Petit Mangeur de Coeurs-Saignants/

The Little Eater of Bleeding Hearts."

I retired in January 2000 and continued to travel and to write. Micheline had started to write and encouraged me in my writing. She kept telling me to be myself and rely on my own creativity. In a letter dated August 2, 1996 she writes, "Don't get stuck wondering if you are a good writer...just write what you need to write...it really isn't about being good, Norman... who else in the world can write like you? No one!! You are unique...good/ bad are value judgements put out at a certain time & with certain criteria... that changes in time...they are not part of our/your truth! Neither are they "garants" de perfection/guarantors of perfection...just risk...just ose/ dare...être pleinement toi-même/to be completely yourself when you reach that point within yourself...you'll feel very different in your quest!!!! Only you can fulfill your 'humaness'...and no one can really evaluate it as though they were godgiven seeds or criteria---worthwhile or not---this is the artist's struggle!!!!Wanting perfection is in itself a limitation(I must admit that I, Norman, have always been a perfectionist)...struggle, confront this 'limitative' desire--transcend, go beyond---write about it if you must!!!! Suffer but not uselessly..." I knew deep down that she knew what suffering for one's artistic endeavor was and I understood her plight as a creator and artist. Except her suffering came primarily from her difficulty of earning a living off one's art.

As you can see Micheline and I were close friends as artists and we shared the same views, the same philosophy of creativity and the same passion for art be it in the plastic arts or the written arts/literature. Creativity is not romantic feely-feely stuff nor is it a gift from the gods. It's a self proclaiming and self-daunting commitment one makes to oneself while rejecting the self-abasing withered laurels of a shouting crowd crowning a poet in disrepute or a painter in total abhorrence of what is spectacular. The spectacle is over when the fat lady sings. Micheline and I never sang lugubrious songs and we never feared the dawning of creativity. Over and over again I could hear her shout, Fais ton excité! Vivre c'est d'être excité à la vie/Raise hell. Living is to be full of life .

Like Micheline, I proclaim the notion of creativity with shouts of joy and a shout of splendor. Splendor in the blade of grass or the pistils of a flower is the call of the wild and the call of the act of living. Living is! Living is not negating one's existence as a human being. Living is! Living is a breath of God's creation and creation is part and parcel of what we get to know as créativité imperturbable/ unshakeable creativity. Go ahead and shake it...it won't budge, not if you are deeply embedded in it. Artistic creativity resounds from the bottom of one's soul. You can deny it but you cannot erase it nor crush it even if you try. You can deny it but you cannot render it null and void. Micheline knew that and I know it. As Micheline says, we are all endowed with a marvelous sense of creativity or at least with a fresh breath of creative ability, so why waste it? Why not acknowledge it by being energetically involved with artistic endeavors. At the very least, by learning to appreciate a work of art whatever its category and mastery. I think that there are too many people shifting their appreciation to spectator sports and useless games of money-making ideas. Entertainment is fun, pleasurable and fills the heart with appreciation, but it's not what fills the soul with aesthetic compensation. "Let me entertain you," sings with gusto the young Gypsy Rose Lee, but she does not always enjoy the hard work behind the delivery of her fabled tale. Or does she?

Chapter FOUR :

A FORK IN THE ROAD OF LIVING--
-THE THREAT OF DEATH

WITH ALL OF her letters, my notes and exchanges that we had, there is an event in Micheline Bousquet's life that marks predominantly her existence as a human being. I have talked about her creativity, her art, her determination to survive, and her struggles with finances and her endeavor to publicize and market her art. However, the greatest part of her struggles came when she had to fight cancer. I have kept a record of that in my copies of our emails dealing specifically with that. It's a touching if not dramatic part of Micheline's life, not necessarily as an artist but as a human being confronting the issue of serious illness and death.

Micheline was fifty-seven years old when she realized she had cancer of the vagina and anus. It was terrible news for her. She related all of the pain, suffering, terrible worries and the threat of death to me after the surgery and recovery. It was a daunting trial, one that could lead anyone to loneliness, betrayal if not despair. Betrayal of her energies and stamina as a woman. In her many emails she relates to me that it was a terrible process to go through. She never thought she would go through such a formidable process of pain, despair and worry for every moment of worrisome pain meant an occasion to fill the head and the heart with awesome tragic pangs of the soul. For her, her femininity was going to be looted just like a cache or treasure that one has treasured for years, and her sense of being a woman both physically and psychologically was in jeopardy. That's how she saw and felt things. Not that she was sexually in need of penetration or even desiring male amorous relationships. She was still a woman who was sensually alive, but she fulfilled her desires with her deep passion for the creativity of art. She had had her carnal experiences with a man, a few men, but they were short-lived and not fulfilling as a woman. She no longer wanted to talk about them and no longer desired to reprieve their brief pleasures. She had two daughters, she was a mother and that's all she contemplated and found fulfillment. She lived to live. Not a life of endless desires to be someone else than Micheline Bousquet. All she knew was the fact that unwanted but much needed surgery was going to dramatically change some of her natural functions and even her psychological venues as a woman.

I'm not a woman so I do not know what it means to lose one's vagina, the seat of physical penetration by a male penis as well as the arousal of physical and psychological pleasure that a woman gets. For me, a man, it would mean the emasculation of self with the danger of the casting off or the cutting off the penis. No more erections, no more pleasurable heart pounding moments of sexual arousement. Would I still feel like a man? I do not know. What I do know is that I would feel the terrible sensation of being perhaps half a man or less.

Let's begin at the beginning of Micheline's cancer. In June 2004 Micheline tells me in one of her emails that she had been recently diagnosed as having an anal cancer and "am going into the hospital for investigative exams to determine its extensions, the type (sarcoma or adenoma) and its staging. I will then have to begin chemotherapy and radiation therapy. ..It is very difficult for me to tell you at this time how I feel about all of this... Biopsies under general anesthesia take place Friday, the 2nd of July...anal RMI and total body RMI on Thursday July 1...I know this is brutal type of info, maybe that's also why it is so hard for me to write it down...it makes it even more real." That was the surprising and terrible news I received from her. It made me cringe with interior fear like some kind of beast gnawing at my heart as well as my intestines. I shivered and lost the warmth of my blood. I felt figé/rigid, frozen like broth that coagulates in the cold. I did not want to hear this from her, my dear and closest friend. She had cancer!

Then in March, I received this email, "I will be operated on the 6 April at Institut Gustave Roussy, Villejuif(région parisienne). There is still 2cm of humoral mass and the anus, rectum and anterior vaginal wall have to be taken out completely. I will have a permanent colostomy. If the cancer has really not spread then this operation should rid my cancer. Continue praying. The operation is major major surgery, at least 4 hours and the days that follow are also critical. I am not in a great deal of pain now and know that the pain will even be greater...I hope only to find the courage. Today I feel as though I am disintegrating little by little. Positive thinking after a certain point is out of my reach...so maybe it is important that those who are close to me remain positive." Micheline knew that the operation would be a horrible burden for her and her daughters. A trial of personal anguish and pain. She did not rely on the sympathy or relief from her parents and her brother and sister. She did not mention that but I knew. It was a terrible situation for her. The fact that she did let me know, meant that she not only trusted me but considered me a very close friend.

Just prior to receiving this email, I had sent her this email, " My heart and soul go out to you and I still maintain hope for you. I have been praying every day for you to find the courage and peace within you to sustain life and the quality of life. This is a tremendous trial for you, but out of this you will emerge saine et sauve/healthy and safe. The artist in you will not allow de devenir éteinte/to become snuffed out. After the operation, you will feel pain, but you will emerge as an artist with a deeper sense of vision and color. You will see Courage, mon amie, car je continue prier pour toi en implorant le Seigneur et sa mère non seulement de te soulager mais de te guérir"/because I continue to pray for you imploring the Lord and His mother not only to help you but to heal you. Medical doctors cure with medicine and science, but our spiritual selves heal us...that's what I use to teach my students in my Transcultural Healing course. I still believe this. I was so confident that Micheline would come through with flying colors and return to her endeavors in creativity in art. I prayed to God to release her from the pain of death and to give her the courage to live.

After a very long period of time and worry on my part, I received this email from Micheline, " I came home from the hospital around the 21 of April but have a lot of recovering to do...the operation was heavy duty, the tumor had extended into the vaginal canal and had abcessed and grown so that the vagina, the anus and the rectum have been taken out. Pathology reports come back so that the remaining tissues are free of cancer so there is not more additional chemo. The recovery will be long and la cicatrisation au moins sur trois mois, car la cavité qui reste doit cicatriser de l'intérieur vers l'extérieur. J'ai des soins à domicile tous les jours/the healing, scarring at least three months, but the cavity that remains must heal and scar from the interior to the exterior. I do have home help care every day. The morale is so-so... such a mutilating operation is not easy to accept and integrate. I have un deuil à faire/a mourning to make, and a reconstruction of a new image of my body and many many changes or awareness during these last few months have occured...Thank you for caring..." I'm sure that the daughters worried a lot and visited her at the hospital. I just wish I had been there for cheering up and consolation. What do you tell a woman who lost her vagina and had her rectum closed up. But I knew that Micheline had the strong determination not only survive but continue living a life of passion for her art and strong belief in a renewed self that she had found before her operation. Barriers are placed into our lives only to be crossed and even torn down if one must.

In July 2013 I received this particular email from Micheline as she continued recuperating from her major surgery and assessing her capabilities and strengths. She writes, "I do think my work is interesting, original and able to touch others emotionally. It's real artistic value escapes me...but that is not essential for me. Sa valeur ne pourrait pas être reconnue si je ne réussis pas à le faire voir/Its value could not be recognized if I do not succeed to make it known. Inventing my own salon n'est plus dans mes possibilités/is no longer in my possibilities...the cancer took a lot of energy from me que je n'ai jamais pu récupérer/that I was never able to recuperate. Apparently, this is normal. Je suis suivi toujours pour des douleurs persistantes dans le sacrum et le bassin avec des crises fortes de sciatiques...mais je suis vivante et je prends tout cela avec une certaine philosophie. Par contre je dois faire avec mais sans apitoiement"/I am followed always by persistent pain in the sacrum and the basin with strong sciatic crises. On the other hand I must do with it but without pity..."I am glad to be still alive!!!" She then tells me that her biggest struggle is still being able to pay her bank debts. She simply would like to know how to get out of the hole and she doesn't even believe she ever could and will. "So I wake up each day...I try to get through the day as best as possible and c'est un énorme effort pour moi que je ne donne pas à voir"/it's an enormous effort for me that I cannot bring myself see. I think I have been so self-reliant, autonomous and independent that I do not know how to go out there and do what would need to be done. Socially, je suis une catastrophe ambulante! "/I am a walking catastrophe! It is sad that she considers herself that much of a ruined being. She never was a social butterfly nor a dancing queen, but she had a personality that lit up a room when given the chance. But she never recognized that gift. She never showed her immense talent to reveal her teaching skills and, much more, her talent as a creative artist. "Fais pas ton excitée," her mother used to tell her. Don't show off and don't be wild and untamed. Act like a doctor's daughter, well-dressed and modest like a good girl. Her mother's exhortation was ever in her craw and remained there as long as she lived.

The girls were happy to have their mother home. They even celebrated the anniversary of her recovery and her coming home the following April. They wanted it that way although their mother had no great joy about it. All she wanted was her peace and contentment of being home without "les ennuis de la maladie et les douleurs ennuyantes et si faciles à ne pas oublier"/ the bother of sickness and the troublesome pain so easy not to forget. It seems that pain never left her, never abated and never was replaced by calm moments of reprieve. It was a constant pain that ever reminded her of this persistent gnawing cancer. She used to tell me, "Le cancer va me manger en vie. Merde de pourriture navrante"/Cancer will eat me alive. Goddamn shit of a distressing rottenness. I listened to her written words as if I were there beside her and complied with her distress by wishing I was able to console her with words and baleful eye contact. I couldn't. I did not have the willpower to leave home and go to her. I felt cowardly like a wimp. However, she was still alive, as she said, and glad to be home with Mia and Monique along with the social worker who taught her how to manage her psychological pain. The home health care worker helped her with the management of physical pain while Phonsine, the elderly social worker treated her psyche with tender and sympathetic care. Micheline accepted the care given her and was very grateful of their mercy. After all, she never did get any of it with her mother. Her mother was a hard woman, a woman who demanded rather than give. Micheline often repeated that to me. I just gulped and nodded my head. That's all that could be said.

With time the pain abated, the worries grew less and less acute but Micheline still wondered what was going to happen now. She realized that inertia was setting in. In July 2013, she writes, "During these past months I have come to realize the tremendous inertia, ambivalence...resulting guilt behind my not being able to get beyond survival. I have been able to understand why and how I developed mere survivorship(very good skills actually) but how I am also inhabited by so much fear that I'd rather be a hermit than go out into the world and let others know I exist as a real individual with needs and desires! L'histoire reste à écrire mais le travail personel restant est aussi immense"/ the story needs to be told but the work remaining is immense.

    She needed to throw herself if not completely at least wholeheartedly into her art. Painting was her ardent desire and solicitude. She recognized that creative painting was her talent and her vocation as an artist endowed with the pleasure of putting watercolor on paper and paint on canvas. Paint with oil was now her preference. She wrote to me about her experience at the mairie: "One day while in Varengeville I had to go to the mairie pour obtenir des renseignements./to obtain some information. It had been many years since I had gone to the mairie. It had been completely renovated, et en très bon goût/and in very good taste. As I walked into the main office j'ai aperçu un tableau à ma gauche accroché au mur principal. Je me suis dit 'mon dieu qu'il est beau avec une qualité de lumière extraordinaire...une vraie énergie palpable'/I noticed a painting on my left hung on the main wall. I told myself 'My God it's so beautiful with a quality of extraordinary light...a true palpable energy. I approached to see it better and to find out 'who' had painted ce tableau. The secretary said, 'Il est aussi beau que le premier jour, Madame Bousquet.'/It is as beautiful as the first day, Madame Bousquet. That is when I realized that I had been the artist. J'étais boulversée/I was bowled over. I left the mairie trembling, nauséabonde et vraiment en larmes/nauseous and truly in tears. I did not remember this tableau. An oil painting in the colors blue-green, valeurs sombres, mais un brin de lumière vraiment extraordinaire/ somber values, but a bit of light truly extraordinary, that seemed to have come more and more alive as the oil painting aged. Suddenly, j'étais envahie de la plus grande tristesse de ma vie/I was overwhelmed by the greatest sadness of my life...what had I lost of myself and if I could paint like this, where had I missed the step or steps??"

Micheline followed this message with the following,"C'est à ce moment là que la décision c'est imposé...il fallait que je revienne chez moi pour mon vieux chien, mais pour moi-même et ma peinture"/It's at that very moment that the decision had to be made...I had to come back home for my old dog but for myself and my painting. "I'll be 58 in September. I do not have more time to waste." Micheline left Nantes at the start of July and began unpacking and trying to put order in her things and her life. She did not know if that was the right decision or not but she told me that, at least she was at peace with herself even though the future was terribly rocky.

Micheline's old dog had been weak and sick for quite sometime. He missed home in Varengeville and that caused Micheline to worry about him and at the same time it gave her the longing to return home. Both dog and mistress packed up and left Nantes where she had been trying to set up shop for a new career in the arts and consultancy. She tried to establish her own business after some apprenticeship in business dealings, consultancy and laws. She was really trying to earn enough money to be free of debts.

In April 2003 she wrote, "I let myself be influenced into obtaining un statut autre que le statut de marginale/a statute other than the statute of the marginal. That is how the consultancy was born. Yes, I obtained recognition intellectually and financially...but I stopped painting to put my energies into this new activity. I learned a lot on business strategy, management, marketing, communication, and selling. I plugged into Harvard Business School and stayed on top of the latest research and development. But the more I grew in these new areas the further I was moving away from art, my art. I found myself in a world that 'je mourrais à moi-même '/I was dying in myself and un monde appauvrissant culturellement et surtout humainement/ an improvishing world culturally and humanly speaking. J'ai eu des mois de dépression dit cachées"/ I had months of hidden depression.

101

It did not work. Not her attempts at business. Her heart was evidently in her creative art. She had soon realized that art was her "business" and her calling as a talented woman. Home for her was her art and Varengeville. She could not deny this and so she moved home and settled down one more time. However, she still had to find the money to live there and pay her debts. She was once more in a position where she stood to lose her shirt, as she told me. It must have been a terrible situation to find yourself in. It wasn't foreign to her having debts to pay with no money to cover them. But, everything now seemed filled with anguish and pain. How would she get out of it?

Micheline went to see a therapist. She never avoided the needed help. She was good at that. In France it was part of the social system where she did not have to pay for such services. It wasn't begging; it was social benefits. She had long discussions with the therapist. The therapist thought Micheline was an intelligent and perspicacious person with a sense of the practical. Life had become a long labyrinth of challenges and problems for Micheline. Where to find the exit was the great difficulty. There was no Ariadne for Micheline only social workers and therapists. She had given up on religious people and priests. They were part of the cause of her problems, she thought. Her parents had been clinging to ethnic religious fervor all of their lives and that was part of their problems, she told me. Micheline was not an atheist but her faith in traditional beliefs was weakening. Besides, she was convinced that traditional ethnic values only threw fuel on the fire of Franco-American heritage to which she was attached as the child of Franco-American parents. She admitted that she was part of the culture and found it, in part, enriching such as the language and its history, but she wanted to be her own person not a duplicate or template of someone's beliefs or something from the past that demanded adherence with a passion of some sort. No, she was a creative person and she demanded freedom of expression and belief.

In one of her emails she tells me that the therapist she was seeing postulated that living from one's art was very difficult. "She is right. However, a very important question was never asked," Micheline tells me. "Why are you not making a living with your painting instead of how else can you earn a living other than through your painting et avoir un vrai statut?"/and have a real statute??? Micheline's reply to this question was, "Bien j'ai eu un 'vrai statut' et le résultat n'est pas un du bonheur pour moi. Et ceci est ma vie et c'est moi qui doit la vivre!"/Well, I got a real statute and the result is not happines for me. And that is my life and I'm the one who must live it. Then she adds, "I think I had to go very far away from myself, to finally accept myself." Always a matter of acceptance for Micheline. Acceptance of herself, acceptance by her mother, acceptance of her art, acceptance by others, and finally acceptance of her reluctance to fit in socially. There always was a reluctance in Micheline to accept who she truly was. The self always seemed to be buried in the piles of self-negation and self-reluctance. For a very long time she wondered who she truly was, just a person, an artist or a searcher for her own identity. Does one get an identity from one's family, one's friends, one's upbringing or one's established cultural heritage. Good question. What is the answer. Does anyone know? Micheline wasn't too sure about that. That's why she always felt troubled or unsure about her identity. Although she was definitely sure about being a creative artist. She had that identity woven in her soul, engraved in her heart and thrusted in her entire body by the Great Spirit of Creation. That she believed like a child who believes in the fantasy of the imaginative soul. The imagination is not unreal but real. It spins stories that are the very fabric of the human person. As I used to tell my students, human beings are intrinsinctly storytellers.

At the conclusion of that email, Micheline adds,"Oui, nous avons tous le besoin du regard de l'autre, mais surtout pas n'importe quel autre. Et bien avant nous devons [se] regarder et se voir, pas comme on aimerait être, mais tout simplement comme on est/Yes, we have the need of the look of another, but especially not any other one. Well first of all we must look at oneself and see oneself, not like we would like to be, but simply as we are. "Much of our unhappiness comes from our inability to recognize and welcome ourselves...so we turn to others and ask them to somehow define us and return an image of ourselves that we can welcome...the only problem with that is that the image that will be returned comes through the other person's filter...it is his truth, not mine."

She adds, "I have been silent these past years, but not in silence interiorly...mais dans un grand désarroi...but in a great disarray. I am not capable of identifying avec les cadres de références que je trouve autour de moi encore moins ceux qui sont donnés en tant que 'modèles'. Je n'ai pas non plus de modèles à offrir...et cela m'intéresse pas./but in disarray with the frame of references that I find around me still much less those who have given themselves as models. I do not have models to offer either... and that does not interest me. "Finding one's own chemin/road est assez douloureux et difficile/is quite painful and difficult. I have no idea what is good for another nor how he should or should not act...Notre existence n'est pas dans une dualité du vrai et du faux, du bien ou du mal.. il y a bien autres choses en amont de tout cela. Je ne peux pas me réjouir à la mort d'un enemi, ni pleurer la mort d'un ami, car tous les deux sont des êtres humains, et de les perdre est une perte tout court. Que parce que j'appartiens à un cadre de référence je jugerais la perte. Cela devient enfermant et dans le mot enfermant il y a le mot enfer./Our existence is not in a duality of true and false, good and evil...there are many other things upstream of all of that. I cannot rejoice at the death of an enemy, nor weep the death of a friend, since both of them are human beings, and to lose them is simply a loss. Because I belong to a frame of reference I would judge the loss. This becomes enfermant/closing in and in the French word enfer-mant there is the word enfer/hell...I accept today as never before that my art may not lead to anyone's enhancement. This does not make it less essential for me!!!"

Micheline liked to tell the truth as plain as she saw it. Plain truth. No embroidery, no trying to hide it and no faking it. Just plain. Of course, it all went through her filter of making the truth known as she saw it, but no lies. No telling it emberlificoté/tangled, as we say in French. No adding one's own views or one's thinking on it. Plain truth. We had a lady in our neighborhood when I was growing up who used to say, "D'la marde, d'la marde, toute ce qu'a raconte c'est d'la maudite marde"/Shit, shit, all she talks about is goddamn shit. That meant that everything she heard from the other woman was a pile of manure, nothing else. I'm sure that such a response would not be linked with Micheline. She never tried to hide things nor make things up, She was sincerely truthful, Micheline. The expression back home, "tirer d'la marde/ throw shit, meant just that to say plainly and right on fabricated lies or make things up superbly and even with some fanfare. Enormously arrogant manure, not to repeat shit, manure that stinks to heaven. Well enough of that but Micheline was indeed an honest and bright person who never covered up the truth, pas d'abriage, as we used to say in our dialect. Colorful language our dialect that came down from our ancestors in Quebec.

Micheline spoke from the heart and not from the bottom of her soles. She accepted stories and tales as glib talk but never did she admit untruth in her way of thinking and speaking. Rather she questioned things and questioned people's attitude towards things and motives. She taught me a lot of things about art, beliefs, work and of course creativity. She never understood why people did not tap into their own creativity. Everyone has creativity, she used to say, especially to her students to whom she wanted to impart a sense of truth in art. Of course, she oftentimes felt vulnerable to the demands of society and the demands of a world filled with assumptions and predilections. She claims that she is no model to others but I can claim that she sure was to her two daughters. They respected her ideas, her wise thoughts and her deliberate sense of honesty. I can say that she was a tender, charitable and sympathetic lady. My friend,

Micheline Bousquet. One day we were out shopping at the marketplace and we were looking at the gorgeous flowers on display. I happened to say that I especially liked the huge white lilies with enormous rust-colored pistils. Wouldn't you know without my knowledge she presented me with a beautiful white lily when we got home. I was simply stunned because I knew she did not have the money to afford such a luxury item, but out of her heart she did it and I so appreciated her gesture of fidelity and love towards our friendship. Even today I can see that lily in her giving hand. I may be sentimental but I can see the real sense of giving with honesty in that gesture. If you want to talk about being honestly human, let's talk about Micheline. She had a very long streak of humanity in her. To her being human was being human and truthful about self and others. I genuinely respect that.

In an email dated July 18, 2013, Micheline writes about relationships that I find interesting and very honest on her part. She writes, "I am reassured that although I asked a pertinent question of you, you did not turn away from me...je ne savais pas vraiment comment tu recevrais que je me montre autant intrusive dans ta souffrance/I did not know really how you would receive as much my being intrusive in your suffering. I do not take friendship lightly nor for granted...as I realize that I do not enter into human relationship easily...it is really oppressive for me to be able to trust l'autre dans une vraie relation/the other in a true relationship...I thank you for trusting me the first. I know if you had not insisted throughout these years I would have just faded out of our amitié/friendship." For me this reveals so well Micheline's difficulty, at times, in establishing relationships. Relationships to her had to be frank and honestly reciprocal. You did not choose a relationship with someone because you thought it might be the right thing. It had to be more than subjective and without misunderstandings. There had to be some deliberate acceptance of partnership in love of the person or persons involved. This tells me that all through her life she struggled with the problem of honest relationship if that relationship was going to last. However, I realize that she was capable of getting into a true relationship given the chances such as her relationship with Madame Roche and Ben and Janine. As for her former husband and others like the farmer she did not trust in the purchase of one of her paintings, she thought them to be filled with hypocrisy and game-playing. Deep down she had the warmth of a genial personality to accomplish a good and admirable relationship. She simply did not always trust herself. She would not and could not attribute trust and reliance on herself. I do not know why.

Then Micheline goes from relationship to the problem of selling herself and her art. "Cela introduit mon problème de fond...ne pas pouvoir montrer mon travail/This introduces me to my basic problem...not being able to show my work...today I have been able to unravel and put words/ sur cette terrible peur de me montrer(j'ai le désir ardent de vouloir montrer mon travai mais cette peur profonde a toujours été plus forte)"/on this terrible fear of showing myself(I have the ardent desire of wanting to show my work but this profound fear has always been stronger). "Knowing and finally understanding is an important facet of my difficulty, however it remains intellectual et pour surmonter avec des actes concrets est tout à fait une autre chose!/and to surmount with concrete actions is totally something else. I do not today know if I will find a way of getting beyond this problem."

Afterwards, Micheline talks about her work and her own self when she says, "Every piece of work that I paint is entirely and intuitively representative of myself...like a mirror inner and outer...I do not fear rejection. I am rather accustomed to that...I know how to deal with it... what is felt like eminent danger is when someone is truly moved by my work. All my visceral alarms sound and I feel like running away. It is a source of great anguish for me and an enormous paradox...doing art and being unable to share it, it is paradoxical. Throughout these years I have been creating des diversions pour éviter de m'approprier et assumer ma créativité/some diversions in order to avoid appropriating and assuming my creativity...as a child quand ma mère me disait 'arrête de faire ton excitée' I was hearing and interpreting 'arrête d'exister'/And of course I continued to be 'excitée' being alive and being myself alone dans une grande solitude/ in a great solitude...but punishment always followed...j'avais intérêt de pas me montrer!!/I had interest in not showing myself. I have repeated this scenario throughout my entire life in one way or another..je veux qu'on me cherche et qu'on me trouve, mais ne comptez pas sur moi de me montrer"/I want someone to look for me and find me but do not count on me to show myself.

Micheline wants to draw attention not necessarily to herself but to her creativity, her work, the outcome of the creative self. "But I have chosen to paint," she says, "because I ache deep inside and wish for recognition... the question comes up...whose recognition??? I have been waiting and longing for something that cannot be...a mother's recognition, a father's protection. Yes, I have been able to survive in spite of not having these, and yes construire une vie avec mes propres enfants/construct a life with my own children and yes une vie de créativité/a life of creativity, but never been able to impose my art and obtain recognition for what I do best, what I do the most."

In attempting to self-analyze, Micheline discovers the self trying to come to grips with the inner person that seems to remain figé as we say in French, stuck, unable to move and unable to get out of the torpor that clings to her. "La rencontre manquée de l'enfance est indélibile et a créé une cassure en moi dans laquelle j'ai du mal aujourd'hui à avoir une rencontre avec moi-même qui se manifeste par mon incapacité de reconnaître à sa juste valeur mon travail"/The missed encounter of childhood is indelible and it created a breakup in me in which I have a hard time today of having an encounter with myself that manifests itself by my incapacity to recognize my work at its just value. "And if one cannot acknowledge nor recognize one's own value, then expecting that someone else can is again être dans l'attente de quelque chose qui ne peut pas venir. Alors, je tourne en rond"/ waiting for something that cannot come. So I go in circles.

"How to break out of this vicious cycle that I have survived in," she adds, "remains enigmatic...I know what I should be doing...exhibiting, exhibiting, exhibiting to get my work out of this house and out to the public eye...It seems something so easy , but not for me. Recently I did propose ma candidature à des Salons /my candidacy at Salons, and other collective exhibitions, but all refused. Early in July however I was asked to participate in a fall exhibition not far from Dieppe, yes, I accepted! Once again, on est venu me chercher! En 2011, c'était le Maire de Varengeville qui avait venu me chercher et qui en juin une association pour la mucocividose a venu me demander de donner un tableau pour une vente...je dis toujours oui quand on vient me chercher...au moins cela je peux faire."/ In 2011, it was the mayor of Varengeville who came to get me and who in June an association for cystic fibrosis came to ask me to give a painting for a sale... I always say yes when they come to get me...at least that I can do.

Afterwards, Micheline adds, "Breaking through the barriers once recognized is not so simple...even when we know what needs to be done... there is a certain type of violence that we must accept to do to ouselves...but violence is not always negative...it is energy, it is movement, it is action and not intended(l'intention ici est important)/intention here is important... to destroy. Birthing is violent! Yet without birthing life would not exist."

She adds, "Can we dare to become born to ourselves...Maybe this can only take place as we mature, as we dare face ourselves, as we dare be ourselves and not what someone else defines us as needing to be??? I do not know with certainty, but do realize that our quest is necessary seemingly impossible at times...but we are our own barriers, so it is our responsibility to act...not to avoid indefinitely ..fear and guilt are oftentimes more violent than all the energies we would need to muster up to becoming ourselves."

109

Prior to this email, I received one telling me about her cancer and its effects on her life. "J'avance lentement mais surement..." she says/ I'm advancing slowly but surely...but many, many things have changed in my vision, in my spirit, in my body, in my mind...je suis beaucoup plus en décalage/I'm a lot more between gaps...cancer is a life modifying experience but it modifies your being in ways totally unexpected. We still hopefully have the chance to discuss this when you come in September... you cannot imagine what a wonderful gift that your presence would be for me." Then she adds, "I still am not painting and having a very very hard time with that...je suis rien, je veux rien/ I am nothing, I want nothing... it is just as though I am waiting out time...my days go by, my nights go by, another day begins and another day ends. I am gardening, walking a bit/ je n'ai plus la 'niaque' d'avant/I don't have the drive as before. It is true that this experience has a before and after. On ne revient pas sur l'avant, mais l'avenir je ne peux plus l'envisager en la projetant comme avant/One does not come back to be ahead as before. Many many things make no more sense at all and I wonder why human beings struggle so hard 'to make sense' out of life...is death so threatening? Death is no longer threatening to me(if it ever really was) but suffering is. I have never suffered so much physically or psychologically. Suffering is not what the nuns told me about. C'est inutile toujours injuste et n'a pas de sens sauf le sens que tu inventes ou que tu veux lui donner...beaucoup, beaucoup est illusoire"/It's useless always unjust and it has no sense except the sense you invent or that you want to give it...a lot, a lot is illusory.

She then continues defining her suffering in whatever ways it afflicts her and her sensibilities. I find it very sad and I wished then that I could have been with her. "If in the world there were not people like you(but how many? so few...) la vie serait insoutenable. Merci encore une fois d'être ce que tu es./life would be unbearable. Thank you once more for being what you are...I do not know if I will survive this traumatism...yes, only time and retrospect will tell. I feel something inside that I cannot seem to let out. I feel it is expressive but it is so deeply buried, ligoté même/even tied down that I have accepted(not resigned) cette vie qui m'habite dans une intériorité très profonde/ this life that inhabits me in a very profound interiority...it is as though it's insoupçonable la profondeur de mes sentiments, de nos émotions. C'est cela qui vit à l'intérieur qui a tellement de difficulté de sortir vers l'extérieur /it's unsuspecting the depth of my feelings, of our emotions. That's what lives in my interior that has so much difficulty in getting out towards the exterior...and it is as though it is crying to come out and I just can't find the way out of the labyrinth...yet I think there is/un fil d'Ariane soit que je n'ai pas encore trouvé soit que j'ai laché sans le savoir, soit qu'il est en face de moi et je suis trop aveugle pour le voir encore/an Ariadne thread either I have not found it yet or either I let it go without knowing it, either it is facing me and I'm too blind to still see it..."so every day is one that I go through waiting, waiting for the night and in the night waiting for daybreak."

It isn't strange that she compares her journey to the one in the labyrinth with the mythical guide that is Ariadne and of course the valiant Theseus who is looking to get out. Micheline's journey is not fantasy nor myth but truly psychological touching on the physical. It's a mind boggling situation for one who undergoes the terrible journey of cancer. I believe it is a journey of consequence, a trek of considerable barriers and schemes of the mind and body. However, how does one get through it?

One good bit of news that Micheline got was the news that her doctor, Professor Lasser, at her last post-operative visit when he told her that he was very glad of her progress and the scarring/cicatrisation of her operation. She then said that the doctor had asked her if she was set for follow-up care with a battery of tests to ensure that she was cancer free. He asked her if she was afraid. "Of course I said, yes," she tells me. "Je suis aujourd'hui la fragilité de mon corps...oui j'ai peur"/I am today the fragility of my body ...yes, I'm scared. She doesn't say what the doctor told her after that. She did go through all the tests and with flying colors. What courage and what strength of character she has this woman, this creative artist.

During all of this time I dared not ask her how her traditional spiritual life was because I knew that her spiritual life was not strong and not in line with the traditional Franco-American values. She knew that my spiritual life was a strong one and that I relied on my faith to buoy me up and keep me on an even keel of sanity and good spirits. It was not necessarily because I upheld the values of my ethnic heritage but rather it was a faith anchored in Christian reliance. Micheline knew that and never questioned my faith and my good health. She even asked for my prayers knowing I would respond to her request. However, I don't know what cancer would have done to my strength of faith and virtue-related living. That was quite a trial of faith and courage that cancer had on her. She's the one who had to go through it. Not me. I would probably have gone nuts and capitulated. I don't know. I admired her perseverance and strong belief in living a creative life. Of course, with time things changed, but that's for later. In the meantime, I must not forget about her friend, Janine. In a card dated January 9, 2012, Micheline tells me that unfortunately Janine died of stomach cancer. She was only fifty-three. That must have been a blow to Micheline.

CHAPTER FIVE :

LA CLOSERIE DES LILAS; THE CLOSING

"LA CLOSERIE DES LILAS" is a famous café/ restaurant in Paris often frequented by literary figures such as Verlaine, Gide. Ernest Heminway and Ezra Pound as well as Picasso among others. They went there to eat, drink, meet people and write, sometimes simply to talk with someone and have a drink. It was a small establishment that required reservations for those who wanted an evening meal and who could afford to pay the price. It was famous for its seafood platter known for its oysters and langoustines. The artist Jean-Claude Meynard painted a large "toile" entitled Closing Time showing the noctambules/the all-nighters with their elbows on the bar. Today they have a "Prix de la Closerie des Lilas" a literary prize given to a woman writer who writes in French. It's an establishment with a recognized reputation. I used to go by there when I lived off the Boulevard Montparnasse. I chose this title for my closing chapter since like the painting over the bar, it's "closing time" for this work, my analytical biography of my artist friend, Micheline Bousquet.

Why do I call it analytical when some people might think that I'm exaggerating or trying to be a Freud, an Erikson, a Piaget, a Carl Rogers, or even a Carl Jung. I am not a psychologist nor am I a writer who claims to analyze people. I called my work an "analytical biography" since I am trying to show that Micheline Bousquet very often analyzed herself, he ideas, her work as a creative artist. She tried to reveal the reason behind ideas, thoughts, actions and even her work. There was always some kind of reason, definition or meaning behind things and she liked to find whatever it was and share it with someone like me, her close friend for many years.

"Analytical" is basically an adjective stemming from the noun analysis. The verb "analyze" means to break down the whole into parts and look into the nature of things. To examine methodically and discover or reveal through detailed examination is yet another way of looking at the word. Micheline did not seek definitions of words but rather she sought to discover the reality of things or happenings in order to better understand and know what determined the cause. She was not a philosopher nor a therapist but she had a sharp mind that came up with satisfactory results so that she was able to question more precisely and more astutely. She just did not take things for granted.

I use the term analytical because I thought it fit rightly enough Micheline's way of processing ideas and questions. She tried to get to the bottom of things. She wanted explanations and she got them when she tried hard enough. Sometimes it did not prove to be clear and right but she tried and tried without giving up. What she tried to analyze were some of the big problems such as why do we humans exist, why can't one get rid of fear and depression and who defines best one's identity. Important questions. Then there was the question related to ethnic values of one's heritage. Of course, there was the question of the role of God in our lives. She did not attempt to get into that too much except to question some theological aspects that were traditionally taught in Catholic schools. So, I do not know if people reading this work will agree with me in my attempt to link together biography and analysis. As I have said, I'm not a psychologist nor an analytical genius, but I got to know Micheline Bousquet well enough to be able to recognize her strengths and weaknesses and assess her questions and answers on life, art, creativity and identity. I accumulated over the years all of her letters to me, her emails, my interviews with her and all the notes that I took about her. If you disagree with me then I urge you to analyze yourself the woman who was Micheline Bousquet. You can even borrow all of the material I own on her. I decided to write her biography because I saw in her, in her life, her art and her personality someone and something worthwhile. Besides, I did not want to simply do some "reportage". I wanted to write a biography that meant something, something that somehow analyzed and went to the core of things such as explanations and reasons why. So there you have it. Analytical? Yes, a biography that tends to take shape through the analysis of the artist and her work as well as an attempted analysis of this author and my work. I simply could not totally ignore that part of the biography since it was so closely attached to my friend's being and her work. I think of it as being some kind of Janus reflection.

I do not even know if Micheline is still alive. I have not heard from her for several years now, no letters, no emails no phone calls, nothing. I did not even receive anything from her daughters. I do not know if they know how to reach me. I only wish I knew one way or another if she still exists. That troubles me immensely.

I am up to the point of closure and that is why I chose the title of this chapter, "La Closerie de Lilas" and its large painting over the bar, "Closing Time." I need to put closure on this work and there are many things I need to deal with, many questions that are hanging there in my mind. So, let's get started.

First of all, there are more emails that she sent me attempting to analyze important if not crucial situations, the many reasons behind things, and other matters. Micheline had a remarkable keen sense for getting at the truth about things. She did not care if people complained about it. She accepted complaints as long as they were meant to clarify the situation and helped to change things for the betterment of whatever was in question. She was determined to grant the one who complained freedom of expression. If one wants to complain let her come and let's iron things out, was her motto. That's what freedom, real human freedom was about, she once told me. Freedom, after all, is not license; it's definitely not one-sided only. "I am free as long as I can speak my mind," she told me once at a meeting for creative artists. She also thought that creativity meant freedom and truth wound up together. She expressed to me once on a walk through the Parc des Moutiers some of her thoughts on creativity. There were many but one stood out for me, "The spirit of creativity lies in the act of creating freely and without constraints for constraints limit the act itself." I totally agreed with her for rules that constrain do indeed limit how one acts and creates. She told me that rules are alright as long as they are not arbitrary. "Well," I said, "anything that is arbitrary does not belong in rules, don't you think?" She nodded her head. We often went out for long walks and enjoyed the fresh air of Normandy with its delicious scent of wild flowers and mown hay. We also enjoyed the satiable moments of silence that cropped up now and then. They afforded us time to think and digest the food for the mind and soul. Silence is not void; it never is. Some people hate silence and avoid it; I think it's great.

One very important aspect of Micheline's thinking and declarations deal with the vital part of the human being. To her the vital human part is the body and the senses. She does not take into consideration what we consider the soul as a separate identity. She sees the concreteness of being human which is the body as the principal essence. Not the spiritual nor the immaterial. I believe she was taught in her early years that the material and spiritual aspects of being human were the essential components. However, after her cancer experience, she developed a sense of one-sidedness in being human. That was through her pain and suffering which was intense and convinced her that the real vital element in a living human being was the body. She identifies living as experiencing life through the body. In a long email that she sent me dated July 6, 2005, she expresses her views on this. I will not narrate the content but rather I will give the exact words so that it will be more authentic and real given her own words.(She wrote bilingually hopping here and there from English to French so that it makes difficult reading. I will continue to translate wherever) "Je suis venue au bout du soutenable pour moi et je ne peux plus croire du tout dans un lien au Christ souffrant, la rédemption par la souffrance, etc."/ I have come to the end of the sustainable for me and I can no longer believe at all in a link to the suffering Christ, redemption by suffering, etc. "I have traveled this road and have had mes croyances détruites/my beliefs destroyed as concerns any type of separation of body and soul. The four most followed religions all contain an approach to the body as being quelque chose à dépasser ou maîtriser/something to surpass or master, that its pulsions are to be watched carefully as they are a road à l'amoindrissement de l'âme. Aujourd'hui je suis capable de croire dans une seule chose...cela est que je suis bien et belle incarnée dans un corps, cette matière vivante n'est ni un habitacle ni un véhicule ni quelque chose dans lequel vit une âme...mon corps est moi. Je suis mon corps, cette matière vivante"/to the lessening of the soul. Today I am capable of believing in only one thing...that I am very much incarnated in a body, this living matter is neither an abode nor a vehicle nor something in which lives a soul...my body is me. I am my body, this living matter... "and when that becomes threatened or mutilated through illness and death is near(as it is for everyone of us, except most of the time we do not dwell on this) whatever 'afterlife' there could be, you really don't give a damn as no one has ever come back to tell us about it... you just have to have faith."

"What I realized rightly or wrongly (it is no longer important) that faith is not enough and does not replace living matter. I wish I could have become more of a believer but that is not my experience. I also know today that we can change from all to anything, to nothing in a time-space frame extremely reduced. Living may be after all being able to sustain the terrifyingness of ambivalence of being a mere mortal."

"As an artist we do not easily accept 'mortalness'...isn't creativity an act of conspiracy against our faith, fate?"

"I am finally too tired to use my creativity to express human suffering, en concurrence la mienne/in concurrence with mine...There is so much suffering from all sorts of things in this world. I no longer can live suffering as something qu'il faut dépasser ou vaincre/ one must surpass or conquer..."Elle fait intégralement partie de notre condition humaine. Je l'accepte parce qu'elle n'est pas dépassable"/It is integrally part of our human condition. I accept it because it is not surpassable..."this does not mean however resignation. I will never be resigned to it as part of being alive and human. I will forever denounce it as being unjust, inutile/useless et un non sens/nonsense in and of itself. It is us as human beings who need in order to cope with it, give it symbolic meaning. ..because man needs to give signification to his life, to life. Otherwise, considering that life may be simply a very small passage in a very large and unknown universe is too unbearable. But when suffering has become so great in one's body, you are ready to accept that all of this may have no sense whatsoever and that that is OK too because if you live, you will die. ..of that we are certain. Suffering before dying is just a really bad joke, and I cannot laugh. But I cannot give it any meaning that I find acceptable to me either."

"J'invoque les forces invisibles que je crois sont autour de nous parce que la terre est vivante."/I invoke the invisible forces that I believe are all around us because earth is living. "I can no longer deify as I was brought up to do and no longer believe in the redemption of mankind through suffering. We are not created to suffer and in that understanding, suffering is unjust and we must never be resigned to it through any means, belief systems, or ignorance or uncaring. Death I accept, suffering jamais plus je trouverai cela avec un sens autre que de nous remettre dans notre corps charnel avec toutes ses merveilleuses capacités de ressentir la beauté, le plaisir, oui, aussi la douleur ---mais je ne ferai plus l'éloge de la rédemption---notre corps est ce que nous sommes et l'âme pour moi n'est pas à part mais dans cette matière vivante. Quand cette matière devient malade"/no more will I find this with a sense other than putting ouselves in our carnal body with all its marvelous capacities of feeling the beauty, the pleasure,

119

yes, the pain---but I will no longer praise the redemption---our body is what we are and the soul for me is not separate but in this living matter. When this matter becomes sick..."we can use this time to become/plus éthéré, plus sainte, plus croyante, plus tout qu'on veut car nous faisons face à la souffrance comme on peut, pas comme on veut"/more ethereal, more holy, more believing, more everything that we want for we are face to face with the suffering as we can not as we want..."for me there has occured a disintegration process which has put me back into my body and the signals that I can now begin to pick up from my body. Only after I have listened to the signals that are so evident (but that one passe à côté quand nous avons mentalisé notre existence)/ passes to the side when we have rendered mental our existence) ..."will I try to interpret what the body is trying to send me as messages. Je peux me tromper mais je ressens que le corps me guidera . J'ai toujours mis mon corps au service de ma volonté...sans l'écouter, sans aller voir si cela était harmonieux dans l'ensemble/I can be wrong but I feel that the body will guide me. I always put my body at the service of my will...without listening to it, without going to see if that was hamonious in the ensemble."

"I do believe in holistic healing but to the extent that we are not wholly responsible for what happens to us, so we are not wholly responsible for healing either. There are factors of chance that we too often overlook because they are not always rational...some are but some aren't. We are not masters of the choices we apparently think we make in life...the only choices I have had in front of me this past year was every day choosing to live(no matter what) or die. I do not know how I have come through this time and I do not believe that I was motivated by my children, by my grandson, by my friends, by my faith, by my life as a whole...I just hung in from one second to another hoping that it was all a bad dream and that I would soon awake. As time kept going on no matter what state I was in, I realized how 'little' we are in a universe that we cannot fully understand. In time that littleness took on the feeling of a strange type of liberty. I could live or die and in the end, except for those who would momentarily be grieved, it did not much matter. That wasn't upsetting for me, even quite the contrary. I no longer needed to find a sense to life...it just simply is and I just simply am...however being meant fully being that suffering doesn't allow except for those who can turn the experience into a mystical or spiritual experience. This has not been my destiny. Funny, I always secretly thought that Ste Thérèse de Lisieux was extraordinary and had somehow my admiration. Well, maybe she was an extraordinary human being ..but I am just an ordinary being and very secretly happy to not be other than just ordinary living matter. Je n'épouse plus le besoin d' être meilleure, plus sage, plus artiste, plus, plus, plus...encore moins responsable de ma guérison ou de ma souffrance. Je ne connais rien de la suite. Je trouve de vivre à la seconde prête prend déjà toute mon attention."/ I no longer espouse the need to be better, wiser, more of an artist, more, more, more.. still less responsible for my healing or my suffering. I know nothing of the follow-up. I find that living second by second ready already takes all of my attention. "Life can be whisked away at any second, suffering is a waste of whatever time you have left...suffering psychologically or physically uses up too much energy...but we do not always have the choice of not suffering so we end up wasting probably quite a bit of time...when the time is up it's up...you don't get a second chance ..and today my sadness is at the realization of how much time I have wasted by suffering...and this is what I am up against...the sadness of this realization ...so when this emotion comes over as a wave, I try to fully accept it and wait for it to break. It always does, sooner or later. I try not to fight it as in the past, nor judge it, nor turn it over to life...it is quite strange when one accepts it as being, the suffering of the sadness seems much less , even it no longer has the same signification. Everything seems so relative to le temps-espace/time-space. Perhaps this is just another illusion man creates ...en occurence que je crée moi-même /in the occurence that I create myself...who knows and who cares in the long haul...On fait ce qu'on PEUT avec la vie...point à la ligne/ One does what one can with life...period."

"Il y a un décalage dans nos deux appréciations, mais je fais confiance dans notre amitié/there is a gap in our two appreciations, but I have trust in our friendship…we do not have to resemble one another to care for one another. I do realize that mes propos peut-être difficile pour toi qui détient une croyance chrétienne très très fort. Je la respecte. Je ne peux plus suivre sur ce terrain, c'est tout/ that my ideas/talk can be difficult for you who holds a Christian belief that's very very strong. I respect it. I can no longer follow this terrain/road. That's all. "At best I have coming through this experience an agnostic, and je frôle l'athéisme/I somehow touch atheism. All religions have too much dépit du corps humain pour sa charnalité, sa capacité de jouir/dislike for the human body for its flesh, its capacity of enjoyment…They have tried for des décennies/several decades to regulate cette corporalité, et quand tu vas mal dans ta chair/this corporal essence, and when you have problems in your flesh they tried to make it a factor of sainthood, martyrdom or at best redemption. The basic values are obedience and submission, pureté ou impureté. We are led to believe that a better world awaits us and that God never sends us more than one can take. First and foremost, I do not think he sends us anything…nor does he choose amongst us who gets what talent…la personification me dérange/ personification upsets me, it is as though il existe un Père ultime qui éventuellement nous tient responsable pour ce que nous sommes, ce que nous avons fait ou pas fait/there exists an ultimate Father who eventually holds us responsible for who we are, what we have done or not done… dealing with my illness and seeing others dealing with their illness…we all bring to it what we can, but all of us go through the same emotions…What we do with them do depend on what we believe./Il faut croire que les bonnes soeurs non pas fait avec moi une croyante malgré tout épreuve../ One must believe that the good nuns did not make a good believer out of me in spite of all trials. As much as I tried to go down this route as so many people prayed for me and continue to do so in this illness,/ mon cheminement est très différent …ma réalité toute autre./my way, my road…is very different..my reality altogether not the same. If there is any sense to it, I can only say that I discovered que je suis incarnée en matière, chair et os/that I am incarnated in matter, flesh and bones. The rest is intangible for me and therefore I cannot count on a common repère/ marker. Spiritualité, spirit, l'âme is for me also incarnated in my body... there is no body AND soul...it is just one and extremely basic based on my physical senses , existing through my physical senses, creating through my physical senses, living in a physical world(whether or not I appreciate it is incidental). I feel that I need to find and fully come back to being 'animale' and not to aspire to whatever is not animale."

"I don't think I have written so much in the last year of this passage de vie/passage of life. It is the first time I put down in writing what has been going on interiorly. "

Whew! this has been a real flight into the interior life of my friend, Micheline Bousquet. I feel I have flown over so many vistas of what I call human spirituality or what Micheline calls human soul one with human matter. It is indeed very difficult for me to fully understand her fall from grace or a detour from faith. I understand that severe illness like cancer with its long operation and necessary drugs can be a root cause of this, However, I also realize that ever in Micheline's living is a rebeliousness against her mother's conservative Catholic beliefs and values. It seems to me that all came to a head with her cancer operation that she calls a mutilation of her body. Imposition is what she objected to, the imposition of ethnic and cultural values, the imposition of faith-filled dogmas and teachings, and the imposition of social and behavioral judgements. All of this seems to have shaken her into a being of consequential dimensions that rejected higher beings like a God ruling over her and leaving her alone and uncertain of the future and the measure of living a full life. I do not know enough of psychology, theology, biology and even philosophy to be able to decipher everything she says in this message of hers. I know she must have spent hours upon hours reading philosophical, perhaps mystical and even moral theological books trying to learn more about matter and " anima." I am also certain that she must have researched some basic readings on the physicality of human biology. She was a very intelligent woman and could handle such challenging readings. She had a passion for not only art and creativity but a passion for learning. She taught me how to delve into things and seek real meanings and true significations to questions that I never dared to ask. I never realized that true friendship could materialize and be fruitful in sharing and receiving what was thought to be hidden and inconceivable. But wait, I have a few other emails that she sent me prior to this long one. It needs to be shared in what I call analytical biography.

The first email is dated October 27, 2005. It was after a very brief visit to Varengeville after lunch in Dieppe. My wife and I stepped out of the train and there she was, my friend Micheline with her daughter, Monique. We had very little time together and I did not feel comfortable speaking to her about personal things. My wife was not privy to our past conversations though they were not hidden matters. I knew that my wife was somewhat jealous of my close friendship with Micheline since she suspected some unacceptable closeness and unspoken give and take, not at all adulterous but close enough to be considered more than friendly. I never behaved out of the acceptable mode with Micheline. However, it might have been seen, I always wondered why my wife was not happy with my relationship with Micheline. She never chided me about it but I could sense that she was not satisfied that I was close to a woman some thousands of miles away. My wife tried to be friendly with Micheline and she had bought her a scarf giving it to her when we got to Varengeville. Micheline then gave us one of her small oil paintings that I have hanging over my computer. Somehow I felt that the afternoon had been distant and a bit cold as far as conversation transpires. That would be the last time I saw her in person. I will talk about another encounter later on.

She writes, "Je suis simplement ce que peut-être la souffrance physique et ensuite morale...il faudrait pas m'annoncer dans les mois à venir que j'ai un autre cancer...car là je n'en pourrais plus...mais je ne focalise pas sur cela...aujourd'hui tout que je sais et que je sens c'est la vie dans ma chair...je pense que c'est véritablement la première fois dans ma vie que je me sens en chair et en os et pas dans une espèce d'esprit-âme intangible sauf par croyance et imagination. Ce que j'ai vécu n'était pas de l'ordre imaginaire et mon colostomie et la 'fermeture éclair' de mon vagin et anus me rappelle cela tous les jours. Je crois avoir eu de la chance car si mon cancer n'avait pas été un de mutilation si importante, je pourrais très vite jouer minimisation de tout cela...impossible maintenant et c'est aussi bien comme ça car je n'ai plus envie...je veux simplement pouvoir être en vie . C'est simple, ce n'est surtout plus une prise de tête et je m'en fou éperdument de la raison de notre vie, son destin, son après la vie...tout ceci n'est pas tangible pour moi et au lieu de m'angoisser, ceci me libère. Je ne sais pas pourquoi nous vivons, je ne sais pas pourquoi je suis toujours là, je ne crois plus en dieu, ni le salut, ni le regard de l'autre comme étant important...je ne sais plus et cela me conforte car je n'ai plus à travailler pour être mieux, pour être méritante pour être par rapport des croyances, des valeurs, des convictions...je n'ai plus vraiment à faire, j'ai simplement à être et par rapport à ce que moi je ressens dans ma chair...je ne sais plus ce qui est bien ou ce qui est mal...ma vie n'est plus binaire...elle est étonnement tous les jours par le fait de tout simplement pouvoir ouvrir mes yeux et me sentir encore dans la vie...et serai-je là en fin de la journée... impossible de savoir, alors je prends toutes les secondes, les minutes, les heures...je me sens infiniment plus décalée que jamais et lointaine de même les plus proches...cela m'empêche pas d'aimer. Je ne suis pas indifférente, mais simplement avec une autre angle de vision que j'accepte sans avoir à y mettre un jugement et je laisse l'autre à son cheminement. Le résultat est une baisse de tension, d'angoisse, d'énervement, de colère, de peur. Peut-être c'est tout cela qui m'aide à guérir sans le 'vouloir.' Je suis contente d'avoir enfin trouver l'animal qui est dans moi, la nature de la bête...qui continue intégralement et intrinsèquement ce que nous sommes en tant qu'humain...je suis matière vivante. Quand le souffle partira, cette matière se terminera...et cela me soucie plus...je n'ai pas à donner plus de sens. Alors je dis un grand oui à la vie mais cela sera jamais à n'importe quel prix. Le prix récemment payé est lourd et pour le dire en bon capitaliste je veux un retour sur l'investissement…d'être actionnaire demande que je m'implique à fond…car la vie est un cadeau, empoisonnée ou non, elle a une durée limitée et elle est non-refundable! Soit je laisse derrière moi hier que je ne plus changer, et j'avance ou je reste enbourbée dans ma merde…aujourd'hui j'ai une poche compacte hygiénique, passe-partout et je n'ai plus à perdre du temps dans les WC de la vie! Métaphore un peu dure et crue, mais qui détient beaucoup de significations pour moi."/I am simply what is probably physical suffering and then moral…they must not announce to me in the future months that I have another cancer then I could not take it anymore…but then I do not focus on that…today everything that I know and feel is that I have life in my flesh. I do think veritably it's the first time in my life that I feel I am flesh and bones and not a kind of an intangible spirit -soul except by belief or imagination. What I lived through was not of the imaginary order for my colostomy and the 'zipper' of my vagina and anus remind me every day of this. I believe I was lucky for if my cancer had not been one of mutilation so important, I could play minimization in all of that…impossible now and it's just as well like that since I do not feel like it…I simply want to be able to be alive. It's simple, it's especially not a hardheadedness and I don't give a damn desperately of the reason for our life, our destiny, its afterlife…all of that is not tangible for me and instead of feeling anguish, this liberates me…I do not know why we live, I do not know why I am always there, I no longer believe in god, neither in salvation nor in the look of the other as being important, I no longer know and that comforts me that I no longer have to work to be better, to be of merit, to be in rapport of beliefs, values and convictions…I really have nothing to do, I simply have to be by rapport of what I feel in my flesh…I do not know what is right and what is wrong… my life is no longer binary…it is astonishingly every day by the fact of very simply being able to open my eyes and feel I am living. ..and will I be there at the end of the day…impossible to know, so I take all of the seconds, the minutes, the hours…I feel infinitely more seperately than ever and far from even those close to me...that does not prevent me from loving. I am not indifferent, but simply with another angle of vision that I accept without having to pass judgement and I leave the other on his way in life. The result is a lowering of tension, of anguish, of nervousness, of anger, of fear. Perhaps it's all that which helps me to heal without wanting it. I am happy to have found finally the animal that's in me, the nature of the beast...that constitutes integrally and intrinsically what we are as humans...I am matter and living. When the breath will leave me, this matter shall come to an end...and that doesn't bother me anymore...I no longer have to give it sense. So I say a nice big, yes, to life, but that will never be at any price. The price recently paid is heavy and to say it as a good capitalist, I want a return on my investment...to be a shareholder demands that I implicate myself totally...for life is a gift, poisoned or not, it has a limited life and it is non-refundable! Either I leave yesterday behind me, that I no longer change, and I advance or I remain in the mud of my shit...today I have a pouch, compact and hygienic, passe-partout and I no longer have to waste my time in the WC of life! Metaphor a bit harsh and crude, but which holds a lot of significance for me."

"I will in the weeks ahead give you my feelings and thoughts behind a creative project together. I don't know if it is possible but one of my first thoughts is that whatever the means of creative expression(supports, medium, etc. painting or writing) is used by human beings, we should be able to identify the common streams shared by all creative beings...some create as a result of suffering, some create as a result of secured assurance... whatever the catalyst, it is about human expression and the necessity to express something about ourselves...creativity is not only human heritage but a survival tool for our continuation...what would happen if human expression is lost, contained, censured, directed? What makes creativity a delight and at the same time something feared? Why is creativity, this typical human expression, our natural way of being undervalued and therefore underdeveloped as a value representing all humankind?"

"Each one of us needs self-expression and each one of us is capable... it is less about the making of art(though that remains a subject needing further development). For me working on these types of issues through my way and through your way of expression...ought to be able to reinforce and consolidate feelings (emotions) in others that they too can find their expressions and whatever they can be brought to express has undeniable human value even if their expressions are not recognized as valued art(which is always dependent on a time/space issue that we do not master)...which means that too often art is mixed up with 'une tendance' or too often it is only retrospectively that we can appreciate the original qualities of a human expression."

"If I wish to marry painting and writing in a workshop is that I see these as des moyens pour stimuler et nourrir l'imaginaire...et dans l'imaginaire, c'est l'endroit où tout doit être possible, permis. L'imaginaire se concerne avec l'image...l'image peut être un écran pour l'autre qui ensuite imaginerait à son tour...c'est le fil conducteur of our 'humaness'. Ce n'est jamais une zone interdite ni une zone où doit rentrer des jugements de valeur ni de morale... nous pouvons imaginer le pire, le plus horripliant, le plus monstrueux, comme le plus délicieux, le plus beau...l'imaginaire ou l'endroit où on s'effraye, où on se réconforte...où est la source de vie...on y peut mettre la signification qu'on veut...une espace de liberté...probablement la seule espace de liberté que nous avons en tant qu'humain???"/they are the means to stimulate and nourish the imaginary...and in the imaginary it's the place where everything must be possible, permitted. The imaginary concerns the image...the image can be a screen for the other who then would in turn imagine...it's the leading thread of our 'humaness.' It is never a prohibited zone nor a zone where we must pass judgements of value nor morality... we can imagine the worst, the most horrific, the most monstrous, as well as the most delicious, the most beautiful...the imaginary or the place where we scare easily, or where we find comfort...where the source of life is...we can put the significance we want...a space of freedom...probably the only space of liberty that we have as far as being human????"

"Voilà the beginning thoughts. ..more to come but do remember that you are not there to complement my ideas, but to unleash your own. We need to develop together a direction. A common destination, maybe and even surely divergent roads, but there are two individuals in this adventure, you and I, and all the other individuals who will welcome our effort. ..we all must have our own direction...and that's where creativity becomes important."

I must admit that I never followed through with this invitation to creativity. At one time, I had suggested a summer workshop in Varengeville merging both our skills as painter and writer. However, I did not think taking time away from home would be a good idea for my wife. She would definitely ask what am I going to do over there, I know. I would not have known what to answer her. I wanted to satisfy both artist friend and wife but I knew I couldn't, wouldn't. So the ideas never developed into a workshop. It would have been a marvelous endeavor for me, the writer and for Micheline the painter, and for the students. It would also have been for me a real challenge since I was not French but Francophone, meaning I did not have all the words and the expressions that are native French(although I could have learned easily). I regret this today and I only wish I could turn back the clock and get started on this wonderful and meaningful project. I loved being in France, loved its food, loved its scenery, adored its language, and simply loved being with French people. What a missed opportunity that comes once in a lifetime. Micheline, I'm so very sorry.

My last email from Micheline is dated April 4, 2006. She writes, "Tu m'importunes jamais...depuis quelques mois, commençant autour de novembre j'ai commencé à réaliser plus que jamais par où j'avais passé et j'ai commencé ce qu'on appelle ici une dépression masquée...j'avais une inertie, impossible de dormir avant 6H du matin, des frayeurs dans les rêves, des frayeurs dans la vie éveillée...mais depuis quelques semaines avec une thérapie démarrée en oncopsychologie...je redors normalement et je réalise que toute ma vie j'ai eu des difficultés énormes concernant 'ma place', elle est où? je me sens tellement autrement que beaucoup de gens... j'ai toujours eu un sens de 'faute', faute d'être née, faute de ne pas pouvoir plaire à ma mère, faute de simplement exister...qui parlera de faute va parler de place et la place qu'on mérite ...quelle vraie merde tout cela...rassure-toi je ne perds pas encore la boule. J'ai beaucoup fait de la peinture depuis que nous sommes vus en septembre---55 toiles et dans l'obsession je continue...j'ai aussi retravaillé en coaching et dois continuer car c'est alimentaire...j'ai décidé de réouvrir l'atelier au publc mais sous mes conditions...c.a.d. sur RDV sauf les jours où j'ai envie qu'on visite librement...je te dirai plus tard. Le film que tu as vu sera probablement pas encore en France avant quelque temps...tu ne voudrais pas me raconter un peu plus."/You do not get in my way/you do not bother me....beginning around November, I started to realize more than ever where I had gone through and I began what we call here a masked depression..I had an inertia, impossible sleeping before six in the morning, fears in my dreams, fears in my waking hours...but since a few weeks with therapy started in oncopsychology...I am sleeping normally again and I realize that all my life I had enormous difficulties concerning 'my place' where is it? I feel so much otherwise than a lot of people---I always had a sense of 'fault', fault of being born, fault of not being able to please my mother, fault of simply existing...whoever speaks of fault will speak of place and the place we deserve...what true shit is this...rest assured that I am not losing it...I did a lot of paintings since we saw one another in September...55 canvases and in the obsession I continue...I also reworked in coaching and must continue because it puts bread on the table---I decided to reopen my workshop to the public but under my conditions, c'est-à-dire, c.a..d. on RDV[I have no idea what that means] except the days where I feel like having company more freely...I will tell you later. The film that you saw[that was Brokeback Mountain] will probably not be in France before some time...you wouldn't like to tell me more about it would you.

" Les enfants ont décidé de célébrer le 6 avril car cela fait déjà un an depuis mon opération...alors samedi nous fêtons avec des amis qui m'ont été très pendant ce temps"/The children have decided to celebrate the 6 of April since it makes a year since my operation...so Saturday we celebrate with friends who were very close during that time.

"Je souffre physiquement encore de temps en temps mais je m'habitue et à côté de ce que j'ai vécu durant le cancer et durant le moment toute d'suite après, c'est plutôt du pipi de chat...j'ai une drôle d'évolution dans mon psychisme...tellement de choses ont perdu leur sens et c'est comme si je devenais plus animale...plus dans mes sensations, plus dans ma chair, plus dans ma matière...cela me déplaît pas , mais je trouve tellement étrange de découvrir cette matérialité."

"Je sais que je donne jamais de nouvelles, mais tu es toujours dans mon esprit et dans mon coeur...j'aimerais tellement avoir un long moment avec toi pour vraiment partager et t'écouter toi et se dire des choses que nous trouvons si difficiles à dire aux autres."

"En tout cas la vie n'est pas facile mais elle est énormement riche et je suis contente de la vivre...je veux simplement permettre!!!"/I suffer physically still from time to time but I'm getting used to it and next to what I went through during the cancer and during the moment right after, it's rather the cat pipi...I have a funny evolution in my 'psychisme'..so many things have lost their sense and it's as if I was becoming more animal... more in my sensations, more in my flesh, more in my matter...this does not displease me, but I find it so strange to discover this material essence.

I know that I never give you news, but you are always in my mind and my heart..I would simply love to have a long moment with you to truly share and listen to you and tell ourselves things that we find so difficult to say to others.

In any case life is not easy but it is enormously rich and I am glad to live it...I want simply to allow it!!!

The last email that I have of her is dated September 8, 2006. Actually it's only part of a two-page email and all I have is page 2. I do not know what happened to the first page. I have moved a lot and somehow it got lost even though I was very careful to preserve her letters and her emails. What I am truly missing is an email telling me about her considering assisted suicide. I was shocked when I first read that email and unfortunately it got misplaced and lost. It's a very important piece of communication from Micheline because it tells me that she was prepared to end her life. If I remember there were reasons given why she was contemplating suicide. I can put the reasons together in my mind but I do not have the exact written ones. So I must deduct from all of the information given me by Micheline, especially about her cancer and her operation, what led her to decide such a coup. If I remember well the reason she contemplated suicide was that she had spoken to this lady who assisted people with end of life methodology. I do not know her name. However, Micheline told me that this woman had once offered her services and that Micheline kept that in her mind as a choice. Micheline had even informed her daughters about her contemplating assisted suicide. Apparently, both Monique and Mia had not talked her out of it. I don't know if they encouraged her or not, but that's all I know about it. Micheline even sent me a family photo with herself, some of her grandchildren and both Mia and Monique. They appear to be a joyful group in a get-together.

First there is page 2 of her email dated September 8, 2006. "Pour t'assurer , pour le moment, je suis toujours officiellement en rémission. J'en suis très contente. Mais il est très difficile pour moi de vivre avec ce qui m'est arrivé. Peut-être là il sera difficile pour toi de saisir et de profondément comprendre ..."

"La mutilation physique est une mutilation profondément narcissique." / In order to assure you for the moment, I am always officially in remission. I'm very happy with that. But it is very difficult for me to live with what happened to me. Perhaps it will be difficult for you to take hold of it and understand profoundly. Physical mutilation is a mutilation profoundly narcissistic.

"Il y a fort longtemps que je pense que notre héritage culturel de Franco-Américaine...sa psychologie plutôt nie l'importance d'avoir et d'être sainement narcissique...il y a toujours là une culpabilisation . Aujourd'hui je me trouve en vie mais mutilée...ce n'est pas le fait d'avoir une colostomie, c'est ne plus avoir de vagin. Si je ne t'écris pas c'est parce que c'est très difficile de parler de tout cela avec un homme, car la seule façon que je pense qu'on peut se rejoindre dans une profonde compréhension est le vécu à toi...il y a là aussi...même si tu en as fait un certain type de deuil... une atteinte irréversible d'une partie de nous-même qui va au-delà d'une expression sexuelle...nous avons tous un corps. JE CORRIGE, NOUS SOMMES UN CORPS! c'est du vrai de vrai...je n'ai plus la croyance comme tu peux l'avoir...ce cancer m'a mise en contact avec mon corps, ma matière, la matière vivante...et sa finitude. Je n'ai pas peur de la mort. Elle va avec la vie...par contre je me rends compte que je me suis jamais reconnue dans mon corps avant d'avoir eu autant de souffrances physiques...passe au-dessus des apparences...bien sûr tu m'as vue bien... comment peut-il une Franco comme moi laisser apparaître autre chose... je devrais me considérer chanceuse pour encore être parmi les vivantes... je suis avec pour le moment une bonne étoile , mais je ne dois rien à la vie. C'est bien elle qui me doit!!!" / For a very long time I have been thinking of our cultural heritage as Franco-Americans...its psychology rather denies the importance of having and being soundly narcissistic...there is always a culpabilization. Today I find myself alive but mutilated...it's not the fact of having a colostomy, it's not having a vagina. If I do not write to you it's because it's very difficult to talk about all of this with a man, for the only way I think we could join in a profound comprehension is through your own living experience...there is also...even if you make it a cerain type of dirge..an irreversible blow to a part of ourselves which goes beyond a sexual expression...we all have a body...I STAND CORRECTED, WE ARE A BODY! it's true of truth...I no longer have the belief as you can have, this cancer has put me in contact with my body...my matter... my living matter...and it's finiteness. I am not frightened of death...it goes with life...on the other hand I realize that I never acknowledged my body before having so much physical suffering...pass over the appearances...you have seen me well...how is it that a Franco-American woman like myself leaves another thing to show....I should consider myself lucky of still being among the living..for the moment I am with a good star, but I owe nothing to life...It's truly she who owes me!!!

"Je peints plus que jamais. Je n'ai pas de sécurité monétaire et il me faut aussi travailler. Le coaching me permet de vivre, mais j'ai 60 ans cette année et je ne suis plus capable de continuer et assumer...je fatigue très vite, très très vite...physiquement et mentalement...cela est surprenant pour moi, mais vrai!"/I paint more than ever. I have no monetay security and I also have to work. The coaching permits me to live, but I'm 60 years old this year and I'm no longer capable of continuing and assuming...I tire very fast, very very fast...physically and mentally...this is surprising for me, but true.

"I am really happy that La Souillonne (a dramatic work of mine in French, a one person play) has an audience...c'est un livre que j'aime beaucoup/it's a book that I like a lot...but your writing is a bit like my painting...it is very personal and an expression of ourselves...it may not be able to draw really an audience as it is an expression that needs to find up front another identification that is a strong...it isn't universal."

"When are you coming to Amsterdam? Maybe I could I could come and see you there???"

"I know you care and worry about me...and that you accept that I am who I am...sache que tout simplement tu es avec moi tout le temps/know that very simply you are with me all the time...even if I don't show it very much...et mon dieu que j'ai de la chance de t'avoir et que tu me lâches pas malgré des si longs mois de silence."/and God how lucky am I to have you and that you do not give up on me in spite of such long months of silence.

Well she did not come to Amsterdam. I did not invite her since I did not think my wife would like it. It was a difficult decision to make but I was torn between two women and their lack of understanding my plight. I must admit though that I acted a bit cowardly for the moment but I have to live with my wife and I've grown tired of trying to have to explain things that are not easy to understand and explain. I am truly torn between doing the right thing and enjoying my sense of pleasure and doing what I truly want to do. It's impossible this uncertainty, this vagueness of delight and wilfull thinking. Why, oh, why must it be that way?

I have reached the point of closure and that is the time to end this work with the proper final thoughts on my part. I have gathered everything I could that I had in my possession on Micheline Bousquet. I have, to the best of my ability as a writer, given you her words, bilingual at times with translation, her thoughts and her insights into her life as a creative artist as well as her life experiences as presented to me. I always thought of myself as the receptacle of Micheline's words and thoughts even though at times I did not always agree with them. I considered myself as the non-judgmental receptacle without prejudices without pre-established values of my own that I wanted to impose on my close friend, Micheline. Certainly I had my own thoughts, my own values, and my own way of seeing things but Micheline and I always understood one another one way or another. We never disagreed on anything. At least I do not remember. If we did it was in the silence of our thoughts and consciousness. I never told her that I did not like her(I truly loved her as a friend) nor did I ever tell her that she and her convictions were not part of my understanding her. I understood her very well most of the time. I'm a patient, tolerant and modest kind of a guy who so often uses his heart to judge people and things. I would rather not hurt anyone and suffer the hurt myself. I know I can be naïve and at times too open to believing anyone but I am not dumb nor am I stupid. I know when people try to bamboozle me or pull the wool over my eyes. Then I no longer try to be friendly with them and I try to avoid them since I do not tolerate lies and a lack of tranparency. My heart is an honest heart. I love quoting Pascal when it comes to the process of heart-feeling, "Le coeur a ses raisons que la raison ne connaît pas."/ The heart has its reasons that the reason does not know. However, I do use my head when it's necessary. I'm not inclined to be sentimentally romantic. However, I must admit that I am somewhat romantic at heart. I feel easily. I remember shedding tears of compassion for Jane Wyman in the movie, "The Blue Veil." I had tears in my eyes and pangs in my heart when I first heard the violin play the background music in Schindler's List. It still affects me in some way. Micheline knew that about me. She had feelings and I had feelings. They were very well aligned and compatible, I would say.

With Micheline, I recognized from the start that she too was an honest person and that she wore her heart on her sleeve. She was indeed an artist and a great creative artist who liked to share wholeheartedly her talents as an artist. Not only share but encourage people to come out of their artistic and intellectual shells and prove to themselves that they were indeed capable of being creative. I admired her for that.

The greatest difficulty in her life was not being able to be fully accepted by her family especially her mother who was an ardent conservative Catholic woman who had very little love to show. She was rather a nosy and cold-hearted person and she never ever strayed from the path of duty and righteousness as far as I can see. It took a lot of effort on Micheline's part to try and accept some very hurtful words such as "Arrête de faire ton excitée"/stop being so wild and crazy. To Micheline those were words of harsh discipline. Even denial that her daughter was a gifted and creative child and simply was trying to express herself in some expressive fashion. True love was never part of that mother-child relationship as far as I can see. Another difficulty for Micheline was the fact that she had a hard time marketing her work as an artist because she was ever afraid to confront people and sell her wares. It did not come natural for her although I always considered Micheline to have a charming personality.

To me its was a sad thing to see one's physical and spiritual deterioration from being a healthy person and a person of faith to one mutilated by a cancer operation and an individual distressed and depressed to a point that she loses her faith that was implanted a long time ago and falls into agnosticism if not atheism as she admits it in one of her emails. I believe that Micheline was so stressed out to a low point of being so depressed that she no longer could accept the articles of her Catholic Christian faith. She did try to reconcile herself to being une croyante, a believer but she just could not make herself do it. It is a very sad thing when one loses faith. It just seems to destroy the jubilant and encouraging energy that one has known for such a long time. I strongly believe that deep faith buoys the heart and soul to a level that wipes away depression.

One thing I do know is that I wasn't always there to help her both financially and emotionally. She pleaded with me to accompany her in her creative workshops and I avoided it. She asked me several times to return to France and have long talks with her, tête-à-tête but it did not happen. I regret the last time in September 2016 when I happened to be in Paris on a visit and did not manage to see her. My wife was even angry at me asking me how come Micheline knew our address and the hotel where we stayed. "How come she called you?" she asked with sharpness in her voice. I had difficulty explaining that to her. Right away I knew she resented that Micheline wanted to reach me. I had emailed Micheline before leaving and had given her the correct information thinking that we would somehow get together. There was a certain tone of ill-feeling in my wife's voice. I could tell and I felt very uncomfortable.

Micheline happened to be in Paris for one of her exhibitions, her last, I believe, Bleu sur Bleue to which she had invited me. She had returned home in Varengeville since she was suffering with bad back problems. When I called her, we chatted for a short while and then I asked my wife if she wanted to talk to her. She said bluntly, NO. Then I asked Micheline if she wanted to talk to my wife and she declined with hesitation and a certain disappointment if not sadness in her voice. I felt so bad, so terribly disappointed myself. I did not know what to say anymore. That was the end of our conversation with no plans to see one another since my wife and I were leaving for Lourdes the next day. I felt empty, heavy-hearted and totally dry of any sense of contentment of having talked with my close friend, Micheline. Where was my backbone and my sense of pride when I was faced with such a predicament. I did not want to displease anybody so I was left with displeasure and pain. Why didn't I speak up and tell my wife that I was going to take the train and go visit my close friend Micheline and talk to her about her exhibit and whatever else she wanted to talk to me about. But, no, it did not happen. It was a complete disaster as far as I can see. A disaster of uncared for and untended relationship. Why do we do such things, I asked myself later. Why? I shall never forget that day. I've never forgotten my displeasure and my inner pain having been turned down by my wife at that moment in time when I so desperately wanted her to be more pleasant and understanding of my closest friend who was suffering mentally and physically. It was for me like a slap in the face. My wife could be mean and hurtful at times. And I could be quite docile and ever accepting of hurt feelings. Never expressing my own feelings when it was time. That's what I would call a wimp if not a coward. But I really am not a coward. I do have strength of heart and the willingness of courage, but I do not always show it. I tell myself all the time, that I need to face up to my lack of forceful intent. But that's another story. Micheline at one time insinuated that my problem was not my wife but my strong adherence to an ardent faith colored with a reluctance to deny a strong sense of ethnic duty/devoir. I have to believe her now that it seems so true. I simply did not want to accept that this was my nagging problem. Will it ever keep nagging me? I do not know. All I know is that it's an awful thing to have as a problem.

One last thing. I close this work with a very sad feeling in regards to my very close friend, Micheline Bousquet. That is, I feel that I did not do enough to be of considerable help to my friend. Sure there were many letters, care packages, some visits and other things, but I was not there when she needed me and called for me in her own way although she never felt disgruntled about it. Like Oskar Schindler at the end of the movie Schindler's List who tells his friend Itzhak Stern with seemingly awkward and painful tears, "I could have got more out. I could have got more out. I didn't know. If I'd just..." Well right now I feel the same, I wish I could have done more...I only wish I could have done more...I wish I had done more but it's too late and I am sorry, Micheline, wherever you are. I am deeply sorry and I will suffer the pangs of failure until I close my eyes for good. Failure does not diminish me but it does reduce me to a lack of empathy and trust. I just do not know how else I can express this. As an author and a writer I have to say frankly, right now, I am lost for words.

ADDENDUM :

Having recently emailed the mayor's office in Varengeville-sur-mer asking for information about Micheline Bousquet, I have just received a notification from the mayor's office that Micheline Bousquet died April 4, 2021 and was buried in Varengeville. She asked to be buried there. A few close friends came to the cemetery, I am told. "Entourée de quelques proches," the email said. I had all along the deathly feeling that she was gone and I would not ever see her again. I still do not know if she died a natural death or not. This remains a mystery to me. Her cancer could have reemerged. Cancers never completely disappear. They do not totally heal. I do not think so. So, Micheline could have died from cancer. I personally feel that this is more acceptable than suicide assisted or not. I know she dreaded the reemergence of cancer. Whatever the case, I mourn her death solemnly and with reverence since she was a fine person, a very talented and creative person and my best friend. However it may be, my heart and soul are figés/congealed so that the reader must be satisfied with what I have written. I cannot write more. It's not easy losing a best friend. I hope someday to go to the Varengeville cemetery and pay a prayerful visit at Micheline's gravesite. REQUIESCAT IN PACEM...mon amie de créativité audacieuse.

All I can say at this very moment is that I was daring enough to write Micheline's analytical biography...*oui, j'ai eu l'audace* de l'écrire. Heureusement! Si l'audace y est alors la créativité apparaît. C'est bien de faire ton excité/ it's alright to be full of life and daring, Micheline would tell me. It's all right.

Norman Beaupré

Milton Keynes UK
Ingram Content Group UK Ltd.
UKHW030232030224
437175UK00001B/192

9 781951 901646